WHO'S THAT GUY?

I got myself a soda and some munchies and sat down for a moment to watch a cluster of girls around a guy. I could see nothing but the guy's legs—muscular legs, terrific legs.

"Pretty cute, huh?" a girl said, then sat down next to me.

"His legs qualify," I replied.

She laughed. "The rest is even better. Great shoulders. Great buns. Eyes so deep blue they make you quiver."

"Is he seeing anyone?" I asked.

"Not as far as I know. He just moved here from Pennsylvania. His name is Jack Ryder."

I choked. Soda bubbles fizzed up into my nose, making my eyes burn. "Did you say *Jack?*"

She nodded swiftly, daggers of hair falling over her forehead.

As if on cue, the crowd of girls suddenly parted. Jack saw me looking in his direction and grinned. "Hey, Carly!"

"Hey, Jack."

That was as much as Jack and I said that night, but whenever we bumped into each other, he smiled. It was a small, almost secret smile on his lips, but a dazzling kind of smile in his eyes. I mean, that's how it must have looked to those *other* girls.

Don't miss any of the books in *Love Stories*
—the romantic series from Bantam Books!

HOT
Summer
Nights

Elizabeth Chandler

BANTAM BOOKS
NEW YORK · TORONTO · LONDON · SYDNEY · AUCKLAND

RL 6, age 12 and up

HOT SUMMER NIGHTS
A Bantam Book / September 1996

Produced by Daniel Weiss Associates, Inc.
33 West 17th Street
New York, NY 10011

ISBN: 0-553-56671-7

Published simultaneously in the United States and Canada

Bantam Books are published by Bantam Books, a division of Bantam
Doubleday Dell Publishing Group, Inc. Its trademark, consisting of the
words "Bantam Books" and the portrayal of a rooster, is Registered in
U.S. Patent and Trademark Office and in other countries. Marca
Registrada. Bantam Books, 1540 Broadway, New York, New York 10036.

PRINTED IN THE UNITED STATES OF AMERICA

OPM   0 9 8 7 6 5 4 3

For Dee, Mark, Andy, and Stefan

ONE

THE SIGN ON the door of Shoppers Express said Shoes and Shirt Required. I glanced down at myself—at heels with straps that wrapped around my ankles like glittering snakes and a frilly prom dress that was fluffed up and stiff enough to dance on its own. The gown was the ugliest thing I'd ever seen. I wondered why I was wearing it and what I was doing at Shoppers Express. Then I saw the sale signs. Buy One, Get One Free!

Pushing through the store's electric door, I snatched up a handbasket and started down aisle one. The shelves were lined with guys. So were the shelves down aisle two, aisle three, aisle four—they were displayed like cereal boxes, all sizes and varieties of guys, blond and dark, brawny and slim, gorgeous guys in tuxes, guys standing as straight as Ken dolls and grinning at me.

"Thanks for asking me along," said my friend Heather.

I glanced over my shoulder. She was wearing a

1

very short, very sexy red formal and pushing a huge cart.

"Any time," I told her, then reached and picked a cute guy off the shelf, dropping him in my basket. Quick as a flash, Heather pulled the guy from my basket and put him in hers.

I reached up for another. Heather grabbed him out of my basket. I reached again. So did Heather. I took off, racing down the aisles, plucking guys from the shelves. Heather kept pace. Soon I was moving so fast I couldn't see their faces. I was still wearing the obnoxious dress, but now I was rolling along on my in-line skates, reaching and dropping, reaching and dropping guy after guy in my basket. Always it came up empty. Heather's was getting very full. Enraged, I skated faster, wielding my old hockey stick, clearing the shelves of guys. Heather was right behind.

"I can't stand it anymore!" I suddenly shouted. "Take them. Take all of them. They're *all* yours, Heather!"

I threw my basket and hockey stick at a gum machine, which was full of little prom boutonnieres, and raced for the door. Heather was right behind me, maybe hoping for a sidewalk sale. She didn't pay. Heather never worried about the cost of things. A store alarm went off. It was shrieking at me, blasting like it was inches from my ear.

It was. Without opening my eyes, I lifted my head, hit the snooze button on my alarm clock, then dropped it over the side of the bed. My entire body was limp. What a horrible nightmare!

Immediately I felt a twinge of guilt. Nightmare? Heather was my best friend.

2

"How many times are you going to let that thing go off?" my sister whined.

I opened one eye and stared across the canyon between our twin beds. Joelle's head was a few inches off the pillow, her short, soft hair sticking out all over. It was the same color as mine, red, but cut in a wispy style that made her look young—too young to be pregnant. But that's what good old Joelle was, home from her first year of college and pregnant. I'm seventeen, two years behind her, but have more sense now than my "big" sister will have when she's forty-seven.

"How many times?" Joelle whined again.

"How many times has it already gone off?" I asked.

"Four."

"Four!"

That made it at least eight o'clock. And my meeting was at eight-thirty. I leaped out of bed, stepping straight down on the clock's metal edge, and went yelping and hopping over to a chair where a pile of clean clothes had been dumped. I burrowed through them in search of the right combination for today. This was not how I wanted to start my summer job at Camp Sunburst.

"Don't forget to zip," my sister called when I rushed out of the bedroom still pulling up my shorts.

I spent just enough time in the bathroom to see that my eyes, which are hazel, looked like two scum ponds, and my long red hair was wild with humidity. At the bottom of the steps I picked up my backpack, which I had packed the night before, and pulled my bike helmet out of the closet. Twisting my hair up on my head, I wondered if I could get away with wearing the helmet during the whole meeting.

3

I knew every turn of the back route to Kirbysmith College, the site of Camp Sunburst and the place where my mother has taught since I was four. I pedaled three miles of alleys and yards like I was in the Tour de France, just missing a schnauzer, a squirrel, and a jogger, which, the way I figured it, was only one near accident per mile. It was June 12 and hot. Sweat ran off me. I didn't mind at all when a man turned on his sprinkler full blast as I was riding across his lawn toward the hole in the fence—my private entrance to the college.

But as fast as I pedaled, I couldn't get away from the nightmare. Scenes from it, as well as memorable moments from last night's double date and the prom—all of which I'd like to forget—flashed before my eyes like the splashes of sun between trees. Last night it had been Tim and Heather, and at the prom, Taylor and Heather, and at Spring Revelry, Bo and Heather, and at the basketball tournament . . . well, it was always the same story, just a different guy. Fill in the blank: Whomever I dated, soon dated Heather.

And how could I blame them? Heather is delicate, gray-eyed, and blond. She has a silvery laugh and the long legs and beautiful neck of a dancer. Somehow my chirpy, shy, little grade-school friend had become a high-school swan. And I, well, I've always been more like a friendly woodpecker—a pileated—the kind with the huge red head.

I was thinking about this, the unfairness of being a redheaded woodpecker, while rumbling down the long steps that led to Kirbysmith's student center. I hadn't ridden a bike down those steps since I was a kid and had forgotten how your speed builds up and gets you at that quick turn at the bottom. Suddenly I was swooping down on a girl and a guy with a guitar case. Both faces turned toward me, then the girl flattened herself against a wall and the guy jumped into the bushes clutching his guitar like a baby.

I shot between them, screeching on my brakes, then wheeled around to make sure they were okay. Two angry faces stared down at me. "I'm sorry," I gasped. "I'm sorry. I forgot about the last turn. I guess—I guess I'm sort of out of practice."

"Well," said the girl, "perhaps you should go to the mall. They have both steps and escalators there."

She was black, with high cheekbones and eyes as long and beautiful as Cleopatra's—very exotic looking and absolutely cool. I didn't mind her tone of voice; after all, if their reflexes hadn't been good, the three of us would have been a pretzel. But I didn't like the way the guy was staring at me, looking me up and down. He had dark blue eyes. I didn't like the pause and little smile halfway through his once-over.

Self-consciously I reached toward my shorts. I had forgotten to zip.

"I'm late—what's your excuse?" I growled, yanking the zipper up.

"I don't need one," he replied.

I walked my bike away from them as fast as I could and locked it into the rack that was in front of the student center. My watch said 8:35. *At least,* I consoled myself, *since I'm five minutes late for the staff meeting, none of the other counselors will have seen my entrance.* I checked the letter in my backpack for the room number, then blinked hard. Nine-thirty. The meeting was not until nine-thirty. I collapsed over my bike seat.

Fortunately, wonderful bacon and egg smells were blowing out of the vent from the student center and soon revived me. Hungry, with plenty of time to get breakfast and clean myself up, I headed inside. I was standing in line, studying the menu board, when I heard a voice that made me forget about every annoying thing that had happened that morning. It was a voice I knew from last year's history class. A voice I knew from practices with the girls' basketball team. A voice Heather and I and a lot of other girls recorded on our VCRs the day the television station interviewed him. It was Luke Hartly, the closest thing Eisenhower High had to an Olympic god.

Rumor was that Luke Hartly was training for the Olympics. All I knew was that every time he swung around the high bar, girls' hearts did somersaults. But he didn't date anyone, not really. He was so dedicated to gymnastics, he didn't seem to notice all the babes gawking at him. Even Meg Jarvis, who had gone out with the captains of at least one sport from each season, was still hoping for a chance with him. *O unattainable gorgeous,* I thought, *O gold medal of hunks!*

"See something you like?" asked a guy who had gotten in line behind me. I guessed I was holding him up.

"I sure do."

"In the meantime," he said, "do you think we could get some food?"

I spun around. It was the guy with the guitar—only he had left it somewhere. He was smiling. Always smiling.

"I can't help wondering," he said, "which you were late for, breakfast or him." He nodded toward Luke.

6

"I have a meeting," I replied, irritated. "I thought it was at eight-thirty, but it's an hour later."

"Really," he said, as if he were actually interested.

"Really," I mocked. "Scrambled, please, double order of sausage, home fries." I tried to move away from the guy.

"Hotcakes, that's it," he said to the guy in the hair net, then turned to me. "Are you planning to sit with him?"

"Is that any business of yours?" I asked.

"I guess not," he admitted. "But if you are, you might want to check out your shirt first. Unless you've done that on purpose."

I glanced down. The buttons and holes were mismatched. As if the window in my white shirt wasn't bad enough, dark, satiny purple was peeking through. I had put on my sister's bra. Cheeks burning, I rebuttoned the shirt. The guy discreetly looked toward the other end of the line, but I caught the way the corner of his mouth turned up.

Luke, fortunately, hadn't noticed me, hadn't noticed anything but the food that was being piled on his plate. He was upset because the cafeteria didn't serve low-cholesterol scrambleds and freshly squeezed juice. People in line began to grow impatient. A manager had been called to talk to him.

"I guess he takes his body seriously," said the guy behind me.

"You would too, if you had one like that."

"Maybe," he said, and dug in his pockets for money.

I dug in mine. I did it twice, though I knew after the first time, I hadn't brought a penny.

"Maybe you should check your sock," he suggested. "The pink one."

I don't know why I even bothered to look down to see that I was wearing one pink sock and one white one—I guess to make sure I had my left shoe on my left foot.

"Do you have time before your meeting to wash dishes?" he asked.

"They'll put this on a tab for me," I said, trying to sound confident. I was tempted to take a bite before my breakfast was confiscated.

When we arrived at the cash register, I smiled weakly at the girl. "You're never going to believe this, but—"

"I'm paying for hers," the guy behind me said.

"I've seen stranger matchups," the girl remarked dryly.

I picked up my tray and walked quickly toward a table. "What did she mean by that?" I asked when he had caught up.

He shrugged and laughed. "Would you like to sit with me?"

"I guess I'm supposed to."

He stopped. "No," he said coolly. "You're not supposed to. It was just an invitation." Then he moved ahead of me, found a table, and sat down with his back to me.

I came around from behind. "Could I sit here?" I asked meekly.

He hesitated then nodded.

When I was settled, he pushed the salt and pepper toward me. "My name's Jack."

"Carly," I replied, still feeling meek.

8

He smiled at me. His eyes were so blue they made me think of a northern sea. His lashes were thick and brown, like his hair.

I focused on my eggs, then glanced sideways when Luke passed by with his tray. Jack followed my glance. We ate in silence for a few minutes.

"Do you like to wear your helmet a lot?" he asked at last.

"I got up late. I didn't braid my hair. It gets kind of wild in humid weather."

"Is it red?" he wondered out loud.

I looked at him with surprise.

"Your eyebrows are red."

"Auburn," I corrected him. I didn't like to think of myself as carrot colored.

"Can I see?"

"What?"

"Can I see your auburn hair?" he asked innocently.

"You've already seen my sister's purple bra, my pink sock, and my fly open!" I exclaimed. "Isn't that enough?"

Conversation came to a halt at the tables around us.

Luke, who had sat down several tables away, glanced over his shoulder, then turned back to his breakfast. Jack's elbows were up on the table. He was laughing behind his hands.

But when I snapped open the chin strap and pulled off my helmet, he stopped laughing. There was a strange look on his face. His mouth opened a little.

I stared back at him, then yanked and twisted the long tumble of hair into a quick, loose braid and resumed eating. I could think of nothing interesting to talk about. I chewed and watched the wide shoulders and powerful back of Luke Hartly, wondering why he was there.

"Your friend," said Jack. "Eggbeaters. Is he training with the college's gymnastics coach this summer? I've heard the coach is tops in the region."

"Is he?" I asked. "You mean Luke might be here for the summer?" *Here for the summer like me?* I thought. Luke and I on the same campus—and Heather far away, dancing with some troupe downtown. As soon as I thought that, the old guilt crept in.

"You're blushing," Jack observed.

I rubbed my cheeks.

He smiled but didn't have much more to say while we ate. And that was all right with me. The wheels were turning in my head—I had some research, a little planning, and a lot of daydreaming to do.

TWO

STRIDING DOWN THE hall, hunting for room 212, which had been turned into the office for Camp Sunburst, I felt totally confident. My zipper was up, shirt buttoned, hair neatly braided in one long plait down my back; and the bookstore had sold white gym socks, which I charged to my mother, chairperson of the college's English department. I was ready for everyone, most of all the kids. I love working with energetic little kids.

"You must be Carly McFarlane."

A big freckled guy with light hair and hands as large as oven mitts was standing in the doorway of the office.

"Harry Klein?" I asked.

"Yup," the head counselor replied. "Come in and meet the gang. Everyone, this is our athletics leader."

I stepped inside the door and stopped. The exotic-looking girl I had nearly run over with my bike smiled quietly at me. "I'm Anna," she said.

"Pamela," a younger girl with streaky hair and very heavy makeup chirped up.

11

"Hau." The slim guy with fine dark eyes nodded at me.

"We've met," said the counselor next to him.

I tried not to show my surprise. "Hi, Jack."

He was smiling, always smiling.

"Terrific, folks. That's great," Harry said, clapping his hands as if we had just done something remarkable by identifying ourselves. "Now let's have some fun."

We began our meeting talking about the kids. Camp Sunburst was a free day camp for first- through third-graders, who were being bused from the inner city. Harry, who had just graduated from Kirbysmith, had spent a lot of last semester in the kids' neighborhoods and told us about their homes, their schools, their streets; it was all pretty bleak.

"Like all kids, they're full of fun," he said, his eyes distant for a moment, as if he were back in their neighborhoods. "But they're desperate for attention. And they've witnessed things in their own homes and streets that none of us would ever want to see."

We discussed our goals for the four weeks of camp and some general procedures. Our day was divided into two periods before lunch and two periods after. Anna, a senior at Kirbysmith and an education major like Harry, was hired as the reading and math tutor. Jack was the music and art counselor. I found out he had just moved to Baltimore and was a senior like me; we'd both be going to Eisenhower in the fall.

Pamela, who was fifteen, was Harry's little sister and a volunteer. She'd monitor free play. I was in charge of sports, of course. And Hau, a freshman at the college, was the ESL tutor; he would work all day

12

on English language skills with the ten Vietnamese kids assigned to him.

When the meeting was over, Harry, arms swinging, bouncing along like a scout leader, led us to the driveway where our kids would be dropped off and picked up each day. A few minutes later a long yellow bus, alive with waving arms and legs, rocking with loud voices, pulled up to the curb.

It took some time to get the kids herded into the gym. This is just an opinion, but I think sheepdogs would have helped. Bathroom lines were formed. After that, name tags were given out. Harry quieted the kids and talked about rules. Then we led the squirming troops to the cafeteria for an early lunch.

"I'm glad we had breakfast," Jack remarked twenty minutes later.

Of the six counselors, only Harry still had his appetite. Now I'd done plenty of baby-sitting and some coaching; I was used to being around kids. But I discovered that something happened when fifty-eight of them ate together. They found a lot of ways to mangle their sandwiches.

After lunch the kids were broken into their four groups—grades one, two, three, and the ESLs—and sent to each leader for shortened periods. I did fine with the first-graders, who, when separated from the pack, suddenly turned timid. We played a very polite game of Steal the Bacon. Then the third-graders came roaring in.

Many of them had lost or mutilated their name tags by then, and several decided they'd rather not tell me who they were.

"Okay, pals," I said. "I'll give you numbers. You're

13

One Hundred, you're Three, you're Eighteen, you're Seventy-six. Don't forget."

"I know their names," volunteered a little girl whose hair was the same color as mine and tied up in two fussy ribbons. Janet. Her name tag was in perfect condition and probably would be four weeks from now.

"That's Eugene," she said, pointing to a kid with nut-brown skin and just a fuzz of black hair.

"Is not."

"Is so."

"Is not!"

"Is so!"

"Is Seventy-six," I said firmly.

But Janet was determined to set us all right. "And that's Maria, that's Jackson, that's Keith."

The kids glared at her. I felt like touching the tip of my nose, giving her the brownnoser sign, but then I remembered that I was the grown-up here.

I started organizing the kids for a game of Capture the Flag. Chasing one another on a big field would work off some of their extra energy, I thought. Then I saw Harry coming down the hill from the student center, carrying a large box. A tall, skinny lady came with him, lugging another one. My sixteen little darlings, recognizing Harry as the camp's head honcho, suddenly stopped spinning in circles, pulling up grass, and tying each other's hair and shoelaces together. Yes, for a moment they were almost angels.

Harry introduced Mrs. Mulhaney to me as a member of a church who was supporting the camp; then he told the kids she had brought them something to play with. I looked at the box, then looked at

Harry like he was crazy. It was an archery set. Of course, the arrows had rubber suction cups at the tips, but anyone who knew about third-graders knew you didn't give them anything more than a ball to find creative uses for.

"It's a shortened period," Harry whispered in my ear as he left. "Do it once and we'll stuff the set in the closet."

Well, we didn't hit any bull's-eyes that day. But one kid—I know this is hard to believe—actually got a squirrel, and twice I got it in the butt. Dear little Seventy-six.

Archery must have made a big impression on the kids. When I returned to the camp office at the end of the afternoon, Hau, Pamela, Anna, and Jack were sitting on the floor looking at the drawings done by the third-graders. They looked up at me and grinned in unison.

"I was afraid I'd get the same old stuff, airplanes and flowers," said Jack.

But no, he had gotten lots of views of a girl with a red braid and an arrow stuck in her rear.

"Thanks for being a good sport," Harry said, coming up behind me, resting his big hand on my shoulder.

"Sure, sure," I replied, laughing. I wanted to kill Jack.

I took the long route home that afternoon, riding slowly around the main quadrangle of the college, re-laxing a little and enjoying the coolness of the tall trees. The square of old brick buildings always seemed peaceful to me. Beyond the quad, Kirbysmith sprawled. Newer buildings with boxy architecture were plopped down in odd angles as the college bought up parcels of land. Most of it wasn't pretty. But wedged in one corner of the campus was a little wood of oak and maple with a stream running through it and a bridge. That's where I headed.

I wanted to think about Luke. I wanted to imagine the way he looked and imagine him looking at me with those gorgeous green eyes.

When I saw his body stretched out on the wooden bridge, I wasn't sure if I had imagined that too. He lay so still he looked dead.

I panicked. "Help! Somebody help!" I leaped off my bike and charged toward him.

Luke raised his blond head and looked around quickly.

"Oh!" I said. "Sorry. My mistake." I began to back up.

He turned and gazed at me with warm, wondering eyes.

"I—I thought you were . . . hurt," I explained.

A soft smile lit his face. He rose to his feet. I stared as if I had never seen a guy before.

"Don't I know you?" he asked, cocking his head slightly. "Don't you go to Eisenhower High? You're a cheerleader, right?"

I, who have always said that girls who cheer for guy teams must have bounced their brains out of their skulls at a very young age, was overwhelmed by the flattery I'd just received.

"No," I said shyly. "I . . . uh . . . play basketball. And lacrosse. Field hockey."

"Wow."

"Wow," I repeated.

16

"I thought I'd seen you before. Are you working out on campus this summer?" he asked.

"Yes. I mean no. I'm working, period," I told him. "I'm a camp counselor."

"Wow."

It seemed to be the word of the moment.

"How about you, Luke?" Too late I remembered he hadn't introduced himself. But either he didn't notice it or he expected me to know his name.

"I'm working out with Coach Inyart. He's big in gymnastics."

"Wo—terrific."

"What's your name?" he asked.

"Carly. What's yours?"

He laughed gently. "I'm glad I ran into you, Carly. I don't know anybody on campus."

"Really?" *Thank you, thank you, lucky stars,* I thought. "Well, our office is in the student center," I said aloud. "Camp Sunburst. Room 212."

He smiled and nodded. "Hope I run into you again."

"Yeah." I climbed back on my bike.

"Hope I run into you real soon," he added.

My heart pounded. I squelched all the fluttery, foolish statements that rushed into my mind. *Lighten up, Carly, be funny and cool.*

"Be careful what you wish for," I warned him. "I already 'ran into' and nearly killed two people today."

He laughed, and I pedaled off, though for all I knew, I wasn't on the sidewalk—I was the kid in *E.T.*, riding across the sky.

Arriving at my driveway, I touched down quickly. Joelle was in the kitchen shaping weird lumps of half-frozen hamburger and putting them on a plate.

17

"Mmm," I said, coming in the door.

"You don't have to be sarcastic," she replied. Sweat beaded her brow. Our parents, who schedule our lives as neatly as lesson plans, were making us sweat till exactly July 21, so we could turn on the air conditioner full blast when Joelle went into her second trimester.

"I wasn't. I didn't have lunch."

"How was camp?"

"Camp?"

My sister glanced up at me.

"Oh, camp. Great."

"Heather called," Joelle said.

"And?" I swiped a piece of raw hamburger.

"You'll get worms," she told me.

"So take me to the vet. And?"

"She wants you to meet her at the mall."

"And?" I prompted her.

"She wants to buy you an outfit to make up for stealing your guy last night."

"What?"

"Just kidding," Joelle replied.

It wasn't a funny joke.

"She'll be at Tanzini's. Six o'clock. You know what I've been wondering," Joelle said, covering the hamburger with plastic wrap, then slipping the dish into the refrigerator. "I've been wondering if Heather picks out your boyfriends."

"What are you talking about, Joelle?"

She pulled out some lettuce and began washing it. "Does Heather make suggestions about who you should date—I mean, since she's always next in line?"

I stared at my sister, waiting till she looked up again. She feigned innocence.

18

"You've never liked Heather."

"That's not the point, Carly. The point is, why do you? She uses you."

"She doesn't!" I exclaimed, regretting now all those heartfelt letters I had written to Joelle when she was away at college, when she was far enough away for us to almost get close. "Heather's shy and it just works out that way."

"'Take them. Take all of them! They're *all* yours, Heather!'" my sister quoted. "That must have been some dream last night. Why are you such a soft touch, Carly?"

I could feel the heat rising in me. "It's lucky for you and Buddy, I am." Buddy was the name I used for Joelle's baby-to-be. "Darn lucky for you and Buddy that I'm the sharing type!"

That ended the conversation. My sister knew what I was referring to. Not only was she reclaiming space that had become mine when she left for college, but she and Buddy were claiming money that had been set aside for my own education. Because of her stupid mistake, she and I were both doomed to stay home and attend Kirbysmith.

"I guess you'll be wanting your hamburger early tonight," she said, her face pale. "What would you like with it?"

"Nothing. I'm eating at the mall." I walked out of the kitchen and stomped up the stairs, wishing that we didn't have to fight every time we talked—wishing that when we fought, we didn't have to say such true and painful things.

THREE

As soon as my father came home with one of the cars, I jumped in and headed for the mall. I had been meeting Heather at Tanzini's since we were in elementary school. The shop sold leotards, tights, and shoes to dancers—and to anyone who wanted to look like one. Last winter Heather talked me into trying on a skimpy leotard. "My, aren't you a strong one," the store clerk had remarked. Standing next to Heather, I'd looked like the dance partner who is supposed to do the lifts.

Tonight Heather stood in the middle of the store, seeming very uncertain. She didn't see me enter and was too preoccupied to notice me following her over to the counter.

"I'd like to return these, please," she said in a hushed voice.

"Return them!" I blurted. "Why?"

She and the clerk turned quickly, Heather's gray eyes round with surprise, her cheeks spotted with pink.

20

"I mean, Heather, we spent two and a half hours in here last week selecting those 'tards."

She nodded, then quickly looked away. "I know," she said quietly, "but when am I going to wear them?"

"When you dance?" I suggested.

She shook her head. "I didn't make it."

"Didn't make it . . . the Karpov Troupe?" My heart sank. I knew how much she wanted to be part of that dance group.

She nodded. "I'd like to return these," she told the clerk.

"I'm sorry—she wouldn't," I said, taking the leotards out of the woman's hands. "Listen, Heather, you're still going to need new ones. You're still going to dance."

Her fingers twisted strands of long blond hair. "No. I don't have what it takes. I have to accept it." She took the bag from me. "I'd like to return—"

"Thank you," I cut in, pulling away the bag, "but she wouldn't."

"When you two make up your mind, let me know," the clerk grumbled, and walked away.

I grabbed Heather's elbow and steered her out the door toward the far end of the mall, where the food court was. We walked in silence. Whenever I glanced sideways, she was blinking, her eyes continually filling up with tears. She had been dreaming and working toward making this ballet troupe since last summer. I hoped I'd say the right thing to her now.

"Heather, I have watched you dance for the last ten years," I said when we were seated and attacking a calzone. "You're an incredibly talented ballerina. You have what it takes. Trust me on that."

21

"But you always told me you didn't know anything about ballet," she pointed out.

"I don't," I admitted. "But I know everything about you, and I know you're not the kind to give up. You're just too pigheaded. I mean, persistent."

Her bottom lip quivered and she covered her mouth with her fist. "Being persistent isn't the same as being talented," she argued.

"No. It's a *lot* harder."

Heather smiled a little.

"All you need now is self-confidence," I went on. "All you need is the right teacher. You have to find a good instructor who will help build up your confidence this summer."

"Maybe." I saw the flicker of hope in her eyes.

"It's all up here," I said, tapping my head. "You can do it. If you believe in yourself, others will."

Her eyes told me that she wanted this to be true. "How do you know these things, Carly?"

I burst out laughing. "Don't you remember that great speech you gave me last year, when I missed the foul shot in the final seconds of the tournament game? Don't you remember all your rah-rahing when I decided to try out as pitcher? How about the notes you wrote me after all those miserable field hockey games which you and four parents came to watch? I've saved those letters, you know."

She reached across the table, laying a creamy hand on top of my freckled one.

"If you don't keep going," I reasoned, "how am *I* going to have the nerve to, the next time I screw up?"

She nodded. "I guess I'll have to then. Speaking of screwups," she said softly. "About Tim."

22

I waved him aside with a flick of stringy calzone cheese.

"No, listen," she insisted. "I called him this morning and took back my invitation. Last night, when I asked him over to my place, I thought it would be fun for all three of us to hang out at the pool Saturday. But I called him this morning and told him it was just us girls."

"But he'll be so disappointed," I protested.

She looked at me surprised.

No, I hadn't lost my mind, but it had occurred to me that if Heather went after Tim, I was free to pursue Luke.

"Well, he did sound disappointed," she admitted with a little shrug of her shoulders.

Like there was a guy on this earth who wouldn't be? Heather has a small but beautiful pool where her stepfather entertains clients and her mother's friends gather to talk artsy-fartsy stuff. There's a great stereo system. There's a stocked refrigerator. And Heather wears a small but beautiful bathing suit.

"Invite him again," I urged her. "Joelle has another doctor's appointment Saturday, and I have to take her. At least you'll have somebody to hang out with."

She looked at me curiously. "Do you still like Tim?"

A trick question. If I said no, she'd lose interest. I had to give her enough room to maneuver, as well as the security of believing I still wanted him. Nothing scared off Heather more than a guy who was really free.

"Sure, I like him. I guess we'll see a movie Saturday night."

She was genuinely pleased. "Well, if you insist. . . ."

23

★　　　★　　　★

When I got home that night, I was in such a good mood, my sister noticed. "Excuse me, but you're smiling and you've got little yellow feathers around your mouth."

"Like the cat who swallowed the canary?" I asked, kicking off my shoes.

"Maybe it's yellow hair," Joelle observed. "How's Heather?"

I flopped back on my bed. "Fine. Great! Doing what Heather does best!"

"Do all sixteen have to come back?" I asked Harry the next morning as the third-graders, wearing bathing suits under their clothes and clutching towels, climbed back onto the bus that had dropped them at Kirbysmith just fifteen minutes before.

Since the college's pool was too deep for our kids, Harry had arranged for use of one at Willowbrook Country Club. I figured the club got a huge tax break or Harry was some kind of miracle worker. The members of Willowbrook weren't famous for their social consciousness.

"Hau will be out there with his group for the second session. If the bus is late, just let the kids play golf for a while," he said, grinning at me. "Got everything you need? What's that?" He pointed to the coffee jar I was carrying.

"A gum collector. We don't want too many wads floating by the club folks."

Harry nodded approvingly. "A counselor who's prepared for everything."

Well, not everything.

I wasn't prepared for the hushed awe of the kids

as we drove up the country club's driveway.

"I just want to roll and roll and roll on all the hilly green grass," April said. She was plump with chocolate brown skin and wore a dozen sparkly barrettes in her hair. In the few short hours that camp had been in session, April had established herself as the "mother" of the third-graders. I wished I could let her out right there so she could spend an hour rolling on the hilly green.

I also wasn't prepared for the strategic placement of two large pink wads of bubble gum on a poolside sculpture of a busty sea nymph. I gave Janet, my favorite brownnoser, a piece of paper and the coffee jar, telling her to make sure she got it all.

And I wasn't prepared for Kevin, a pale, skinny kid who stared at me defiantly when I told everyone to undress.

"Kevin, did you hear what I said?" I asked quietly. "Please do it."

He didn't move. Didn't blink.

Has he forgotten to wear his trunks? I wondered. *Is he too poor to own a pair? Maybe he's simply afraid of the water.*

I bent down close to him. "Kevin, are you wearing a bathing suit under there?"

He shrugged.

Could I get in trouble for taking a peek?

About ten feet away, a guy who had been assigned as our lifeguard was sipping from a Thermos. I walked over to him.

"Excuse me, I've got kind of a problem here," I said and whispered my request.

25

"That's not my job," the guy replied coolly. He walked away still sipping.

"I just thought maybe you were here to help!" I yelled after him.

He kept walking.

"What do you need?" a friendlier voice asked.

A tall, very tan guy was standing a few feet away from me. He was a country-club hunk, slim and outrageously classy in his tennis duds. I was surprised by his offer.

After I explained the problem, he led Kevin to the other side of the pool. Meanwhile, I got the other kids into the water. Harry had told me that most of them were used to fire hydrants rather than pools. Of course Seventy-six—who this morning wanted to be called Eugene, and insisted on calling me Coachie—immediately tried to swim to the deep end. It wasn't hard to catch him; he could barely do the dog paddle. The rest of the kids stood obediently next to the wall, eyes bright with excitement and teeth chattering. Ten minutes later Kevin joined us.

"Poodles," the nice country-club guy said, bending down to me at the pool's edge. His sun-streaked hair fell forward. His eyes wandered from my face and rested very comfortably below my shoulders. "The problem was red shorts with white poodles. I got him another pair at the Lost and Found, but they're a little big."

In truth, we could have pumped up those trunks for a flotation device, but I was extremely grateful to the guy. "Thanks. Thanks a lot."

"My name's Steve," he said. "And yours—I know you're a member here—you look so familiar, but—"

"Sorry, no. I'm just here with the camp."

I turned back to the kids.

"So what's your name, camper?"

"Carly." I smiled over my shoulder. "It's nice to meet you—I've got to teach now."

We spent the lesson playing games, which is what I'd planned: one activity after another that was too much fun for even the most timid kids to notice that the water was touching their lips and splashing up over their noses.

By the time I had them out of the pool again, wrapped in towels and lined up on two benches, I had completely forgotten about Steve. Then I saw skinny Kevin waving shyly and felt a hand on my arm.

"I remember you now," said Steve. "Carly McFarlane. You were a Pony-Girl or something like that. You were leader of the pack on the playground in third grade."

I blinked up at him and blushed. My third-grader campers looked on with interest.

He took off his sunglasses. "My last name's Dulaney. In fourth grade I transferred to Worthington Prep, so maybe you don't remember. . . ."

"Steven Dulaney? I remember. It's just that—it's just that you look so—so different," I stammered. *So much better,* I thought. A thousand times better! His pale mousy hair had turned sun gold. His wimpy face had miraculously filled out. Bony shoulders had somehow become broad; his arms and legs were lean but muscular, from tennis I guessed. Most of all, he didn't look like he was about to cry at any moment. *People really do grow up,* I thought. There was hope for us all. "You look great!" I gushed.

27

He smiled back. "You look exactly the same."

"Uh, thanks."

"Isn't she taller?" asked Eugene.

"I was trying to remember," Steve said, toying with his designer sunglasses. I could see my reflection in them: my drying hair, though braided, was springing out like wildfire. "Didn't you have a close friend, a girl named Heather?"

"Yeah. We're still best friends."

"You are? Would I recognize her now?"

"She's still gorgeous," I said.

Then the mental wheels started turning. Heather would be occupied by Tim this week, and maybe even next week, if he didn't come on too strong. But then what? Tim, who thought classical music was the stuff Vanessa Williams sang, was hardly Heather's type; she liked him only because I did. But what if I found the perfect match for her? Steve, with his good looks and money and preppy style, might be it. If I was really lucky, he might even have an artsy-fartsy streak in him. This was worth investigating.

"We should get together some time," I suggested, "you, me, and Heather." But before I could jot down my phone number, I saw Harry coming toward us. "Oops, here comes Camp Sunburst. Got to pick up my next session. I'm here in the morning," I said quickly, "and at Kirbysmith every afternoon."

Steve slipped on his shades. "I'll be in touch."

He didn't waste any time.

"You got a phone message," Jack said when I met him and Anna at lunch that day. The three of us were

28

a team, assigned to alternate with Harry, Hau, and Pamela as lunchtime monitors.

"A message?" I held out my hand expectantly.

"Sorry. I left it on the bulletin board at the office."

I nodded and started moving away from him. I had my eye on the third-graders: several of them were sitting with their heads close together, like little conspirators.

"How do you know Steve Dulaney?" Jack called across two tables.

"What?"

"Steve Dulaney. He's hoping you and Heather are free Thursday night."

"You read my message?" I exclaimed.

Out of the corner of my eye I saw two innocent first-graders passing squeeze bottles of ketchup over to the third-graders, who already had more ketchup than they needed. Anna and I each snagged a bottle and set them back where they belonged.

"I answered the phone," Jack explained. "Steve's having a party. Thursday night. He said to come anytime after eight-thirty. There will be lots of people there."

"I'm surprised you didn't invite yourself."

"Didn't have to," Jack replied easily. "He asked me last week."

"Oh."

"I live next door to Steve."

"Oh."

He put his hand on the shoulder of a second-grader who was dueling the kids on either side of him with a plastic knife. "If you get your eyes poked out, Franklin," Jack said, "how are you going to draw all those great pictures?" Then he turned back to me. "Who's Heather?"

"Heather?" *Well, well,* I thought. One more for the list—Tim, Steve, Jack—and Jack was a real musical, artistic type. He could be the perfect match. The only problem was that I didn't want Heather anywhere near campus; I didn't want her hanging out anywhere close to the gym where Luke worked out. Well, during the day she'd probably be at a dance studio halfway across the city. Maybe she and Jack would see each other only at night.

"I'll introduce you to her at the party," I told him. "I know you'll like her. She's really gorgeous."

He laughed, then grew suddenly alert. "Eugene!"

Number Seventy-six was armed and dangerous, launching carrot sticks dipped in ketchup with a rubber band. He made several direct strikes before the second-graders organized a counterattack. They didn't have much left on their trays—just bowls of applesauce, which were quickly pushed toward a kid wearing a baseball cap. I raced around the third-grade table, making a play for Eugene's stockpile of carrots, certain that the second-graders wouldn't have the guts to fire.

Wrong. Wrong twice. *Splat! Splat!* Applesauce ran down my cheek and arm.

"You! Kid!" hollered Eugene, who never missed an opportunity. "You just hit Coachie." He had the squeeze bottle in his hand, eager to wreak revenge in my name, but Jack was right behind him, ready to snatch the ketchup out of his hand.

"Whoops!" Jack said. "Sorry."

"Oh!" I ducked a second too late. "*Ohhh!*"

Cold, oozy stuff clung to my cheeks. Fifty-eight voices fell silent. Quiet rolled like a tide to far corners of the food hall. I stood still, bleeding ketchup down one side of my face, dropping globs of applesauce from the other. Jack buried his chin in his chest and peeked up at me, making little coughing noises. I could see his shoulders shaking.

The little kids blinked their eyes. They couldn't hold it in. A first-grader let out a squeal, and the rest shrieked with laughter.

Harry, who had witnessed the scene from the cafeteria doorway, quickly escorted out Eugene and Terry, the kid who had pitched the applesauce.

"Why don't you take Jack too?" I muttered, which broke the straight face Harry was trying to keep.

"I couldn't help it, Carly. It slipped," Jack insisted.

Only Anna didn't smile—but her eyes were dancing.

"Here," Jack said, his voice trembling with suppressed laughter, "let me clean you off."

"I can take care of myself, thank you."

"Now don't be mad, Carly." His voice was quiet and easy, as if he were soothing a child. "I've got an extra T-shirt in my backpack. Want to borrow it?"

"Thanks—I'd rather attract bees all afternoon."

He shrugged. "Okay. Have it your way." He held out a stack of napkins.

I snatched them and strode off with as much dignity as I could muster. I didn't get far.

"Carly, hi!" Luke said.

Oh, no.

"How's it going?" he asked, his green eyes shining.

His teammates—they had to be a gymnastics team, why else would seven bodies-to-die-for wearing sexy towels around sweating necks happen to be standing together in the food line—were staring at me and snickering.

"Great," I said. "How's your day been?"

He smiled. "Really good. Coach is helping me be the best I can be."

"Glad to hear it."

From the other side of the table, Jack was watching me curiously. The oozy stuff was starting to congeal. I wanted to slither away while I could.

Then Luke surprised me. He took a step toward me, hesitated, and took another. He slowly removed the towel from his neck. It was all I could do not to stare at his throat, at the way his chest and shoulders seemed to surge up under his sleeveless shirt. Very, very gently, he wiped my cheek, my neck, my arm. I wished the kids had thrown more.

"There you go. Better?"

"Yeah," I said breathlessly. "Thanks."

He folded the towel neatly and placed it in my hands. I wondered if I'd have to give it back some day.

"See ya around," Luke said, smiling sweetly at me.

I stared after him as he made his way back to the food line.

A moment later, Jack walked past me, smirking. "Some bee," he said.

FOUR

TERRY, THE KID who had pitched the applesauce, inspired me. That afternoon, when the second-graders showed up, I got out the T-ball set. The kids loved the old gloves that the church had collected for them, some of them punching them with their fists like big leaguers, others wearing them as hats. They came up to the plate and wheeled around like little windmills, smacking the ball off the tee.

When it was time to clean up, I was missing one ball, the one I had hit. The kids scattered to look, then Miguel called from beyond third base. He was well past the edge of the field, next to a stand of bushy pines. "Miss Carly!" he hollered, then threw a bullet to home plate that stunned me.

When I returned to the camp office at the end of the day, I told Anna and Hau about Miguel's incredible throw.

They looked at each other.

"You should let him know it was incredible," Hau said.

Anna nodded. "We were just talking about Miguel. We think he has a really tough situation at home. There's probably some abuse, though we don't have any evidence that it's physical. Verbal or physical—he could use a lot of praise."

"They all could," Harry said, coming through the office door. "Even Eugene—if only he would give us something to praise him about. Carly, here's a note of apology from your pal."

I unfolded a piece of paper that had been creased many times and read it aloud.

Dere Coachiey,
    I am sory I got you wit the catchup.
    I gues I am sory about the appelsause, to.
    I wil trie not to laughff at you so loud again.
    But you lookd funney.
                Your fiend,
                Eugene, 76

"And here's a note from Terry," said Harry.

"How about one from Jack?" I asked. He had come in with Harry and was unloading a small cart stacked with books, brushes, paints, macaroni, cereal, and a CD player.

One side of Jack's mouth drew up. "You're not very grateful," he observed. "I bet Eggbeaters—"

"His name is Luke."

"—wouldn't even have noticed you wearing the beard of applesauce. It was the red ketchup that made you stand out."

"Sure wish he'd notice me," Pamela sighed. She

34

was camped out in her brother's chair, filing a nail she had broken on the playground.

"Speaking of guys who notice—" Jack reached over to the bulletin board and untacked a pink slip of paper. "Your phone message," he said to me. "They're lining up. I think even 'your *fiend*,' Eugene, has a crush on you."

I took the paper without saying anything. I knew he was just teasing, but I was feeling a little sensitive about my track record with guys these days.

"Well," I said, reaching for my bike helmet. "I've got to stop at a friend's on the way home, and I need to get out of this shirt before I start smelling like a compost heap."

Jack caught me lightly by the arm, then thrust a T-shirt in my hands. "Put it on. Don't be so stubborn, Carly. You'll be a lot more comfortable."

Well, I didn't want to show up at Heather's house smelling like garbage, and I'd never squeeze into one of her tops, so I accepted the shirt. Ten minutes later, after scrubbing down my skin, then unbraiding and rinsing out clumps of sticky hair, I returned to the office. I kept sniffing. It was faint, yet I was very aware of the smell—a kind of herbal scent, but very masculine. A good smell, one I liked having close to me. I lifted the neck of the shirt up to my nose.

"I wore it for forty minutes in air-conditioning," Jack said defensively.

I hadn't seen him sitting inside the office. Everyone else had left. Quickly I pulled the shirt down. "It's . . . uh . . . nice and soft. Thanks for letting me borrow it."

"You're welcome." He was staring at my hair. It was doing its damp frizz thing.

"I can't help it," I said, quickly reaching up, sounding as defensive as he had. "This is the way it grows."

He smiled at me and kept smiling until I glanced away. Then he finished counting up sheets of colored paper.

When he had set them aside, I said, "I noticed that you didn't show everyone what the third-graders painted this afternoon. And I bet I know the subject."

He laughed. "The kids are fascinated by you. What's so bad about that?"

"Nothing, it's just that—" I bit my tongue.

"What?" he asked.

"Never mind."

"What?" he asked again softly.

"I don't know. Sometimes I wish I was a different kind of person," I mumbled. "Well, I've got to go now."

"Any particular kind of different?"

"Delicate," I replied immediately.

Jack tried to stop his laugh and ended up snorting. "Sorry," he said and cleared his throat. "Sorry. Okay. . . . Delicate."

"Like a dancer. And maybe blond."

He nodded, then glanced past me. "Would you like straight blond hair?"

"Yeah. Yellow hair that hangs like silk."

"And maybe you'd be a couple inches shorter," he suggested.

I popped on my helmet. "Absolutely. That way I wouldn't tower over any guys."

"And you'd probably walk around in a leotard and very short skirt."

I sighed. "You've got it."

"Carly, I think someone's looking for you. Just a wild guess, but I think it's Heather."

I glanced out the door. "Heather! What are you doing here?"

"Carly, I've got the greatest news!" she said, rushing down the hall toward me, wearing a leotard and very short skirt. "Wait till you hear—you'll never believe it! I took your advice."

"Yeah?"

"I talked with some people who know about dance," she said as she came into the office. "And then I signed up. I'm taking lessons from Françoise Bui. *The* Françoise Bui. Right here on campus!"

"Right here on campus?" I repeated, a sinking feeling in my stomach.

"You know the Hughes Building?"

I knew it all right.

"It's connected to the new gym," Heather rushed on. "And you'll never, never, never guess who I saw there."

"Let me try," Jack volunteered.

Heather turned her large gray eyes on him, then moved closer to me. "Who's that?"

"Just Jack."

"Call me 'Just' for short," he said, rocking back in his chair.

I rolled my eyes.

Heather laid her hand on my arm. "I saw . . . are you ready? You're not going to believe it."

"Luke Hartly," we said at the same time.

She looked disappointed. "You knew he was here? Carly, why didn't you tell me?"

I sat down on a desktop and started playing with Harry's pens. "I—I guess it slipped my mind."

Now it was Jack's turn to roll his eyes. Fortunately, Heather didn't see him. I've never lied to her before and now I had done it twice in two days. I felt like a rat.

"Isn't it funny, how we all ended up on campus together?" she said wonderingly.

"Yeah, funny," I replied. "Glad I gave such good advice. Listen, Heather, I've got some news too. Do you remember Steve Dulaney?"

"Steve Dulaney. . . ." She walked around in slow circles. Jack eyed her perfect legs and shapely little behind.

"We knew him in third grade," I reminded her.

She shook her head and frowned.

"Anyway, he invited us to a party."

Heather cocked her head. "Wait a minute. Steve Dulaney—that skinny little nerd?"

"Well—"

"Why is that good news?" she asked.

"Well, he's changed, and I think he's kind of nice—and he remembered you."

She pulled herself up gracefully on a tall stool. Jack watched her appreciatively.

"How could he forget either of us, Carly?" Heather asked. "Remember the day we snatched his belt while he was in gym class and he was too afraid to say anything, and right in the middle of the spelling bee his pants fell down?"

"But he's filled out a lot," I said quickly.

Jack laughed, and I shot him a look.

"Oh, he has," Jack interjected. "I mean, I guess he has. I just moved here. But I think he's a pretty good-looking guy. You should go to the party and check him out."

Heather looked at Jack surprised.

"I'm going," he added.

She bit her lip and glanced at me.

Jack smiled and rose from his chair. "Nice meeting you," he told Heather. "See you tomorrow, Carly," he said, knocking twice on my helmet.

When he was gone, Heather focused on me. "Why didn't you mention Luke?" she asked.

"I just told you," I whined, not wanting to repeat the lie.

"And why," she glanced at the door through which Jack had just exited, "didn't you mention *him?*"

Thursday night I walked into Steve Dulaney's party and turned heads. Okay, Heather turned heads, but I was standing right next to her. Seeing all those cute guys, I actually forgot my mission: for thirty seconds, I completely forgot about Luke.

Then Steve stepped forward. Once he got ahold of Heather's hand, he wouldn't let go. I smiled, ignoring Heather's panicked looks, and set off on my campaign.

Normally, I would have felt out of place at a party like that. Steve's friends fit the two types of prep-school kids that I avoided. The first were the straight arrows, the kids who dressed like they were clones of their parents in expensive, dry-clean-only sports clothes that you'd never play a real sport in.

39

The second type were all the preps who rebelled by spending big bucks on grunge dress (the grunge dressers never drive grunge cars, however). I usually avoided those kinds, but I discovered that night that some of them were really nice. Having a mission, I had to plunge right in, and I met a lot of friendly guys. We were interested in the same things—athletics and Heather.

After an hour and a half of circulating through the first floor, I realized I hadn't run into Jack, which was just as well. I suspected he knew what I was up to, and I wasn't in the mood for teasing. I got myself a soda and some munchies and sat down for a moment to watch a cluster of girls around a guy. I could see nothing but the guy's legs—muscular legs, terrific legs, legs that would look great with Heather if the rest of him matched up.

"Pretty cute, huh?" a girl said, then sat down next to me. She was a grunge accessorized by a sports watch that had enough stuff on it to navigate across the South Pole.

"His legs qualify," I replied.

She laughed. "The rest is even better. Great shoulders. Great buns. Eyes so deep blue they make you quiver."

"Is he seeing anyone?" I asked.

"Not as far as I know. He just moved here from Pennsylvania. His name is Jack Ryder."

I choked. Soda bubbles fizzed up into my nose, making my eyes burn. "Did you say *Jack?*"

She nodded swiftly, daggers of hair falling over her forehead. "I think he lives next door."

As if on cue, the crowd of girls suddenly parted.

40

Jack saw me looking in his direction and grinned. "Hey, Carly!"

"Hey, Jack."

"You know him?" breathed the girl next to me.

The others stared at me, then glanced at each other.

Later that evening, when I thought about it, it was pretty funny. All Jack did was say two words of greeting and flash a bright smile, but he may as well have crowned me homecoming queen. Suddenly, all the girls wanted to talk to me.

The rest of the night was very busy. While I was trying to interview guys for Heather, the girls were questioning me about Jack. It just goes to show how popular you can be when you've got the right connections.

"Looks like you're having a great time," Jack observed when I ran into him in the kitchen.

"Yup. How about you?"

He nodded. "Pretty good. I like meeting people."

I saw him eyeing my hair. In a moment of high humidity and desperation I had resorted to the method my mother said she'd used as a teenager: I ironed it. It was supposed to look smooth and sort of prime-time glamorous.

"What did you do to your hair?" he asked.

"Fixed it," I replied brusquely.

"You use a tool kit for that?"

"I ironed it, okay?"

That was as much as Jack and I said that night, but whenever we bumped into each other, he smiled. It was a small, almost secret smile on his lips, but a dazzling kind of smile in his eyes. I mean, that's how it must have looked to those other girls.

41

FIVE

LAST DAY OF the camp week! The kids were wound up. The first-graders sang in high, chirpy voices all the way to the country-club pool—nonsense songs that Jack had been teaching them. I felt as if I were being bused in a cage of canaries.

Steve found me at the pool that morning and wanted to talk about Heather, but I had to keep an eye on every one of my little campers. I waved him away. "Call me," I said.

Twenty minutes later one of Steve's friends showed up, interested in the same topic. I told him the same thing as Steve, rattling off my phone number. Later, two brunets with skimpy suits and pop-up chests caught up with me as I was herding the kids to the bus.

"Carla!" the tall one called out.

"Carol!" her friend shouted, waving at me.

I didn't reply. I was busy watching three of my first-graders uproot a row of country-club begonias. I hurried toward the kids, but before I could rescue the flowers, the two girls put themselves squarely in my path.

"We've heard you're good friends with Jack," the tall one began.

"And we've been wondering if he has a girlfriend," her friend continued.

Despite their height difference, they reminded me of twins. They both had perfectly manicured fingernails and blue butterflies painted on their toenails. They wore bikini tops that tied with little bows and had the exact same way of holding their heads high.

"Does he have a girlfriend here in Baltimore?" the tall one asked.

"Does he have a girl back in Pennsylvania?" her friend echoed.

I shrugged my shoulders. "I don't know. . . . Franklin, Noelle, Shane, get out of the flowers."

"Is he interested in dating?" the shorter one asked.

"What kind of girls does he like?" the other wanted to know.

"Tall?"

"Petite?"

"I don't know," I replied a second time. "I *said* leave the begonias *alone!*"

"Well, where do you guys like to hang?" the short girl asked, playing with the bow on her bathing suit.

"We don't."

"I thought you were friends."

"We work together, that's all. Listen, I've got to go now."

"We'll call you," the tall one said. "I'm Sarah. This is Sandra. What's your phone number?"

"I've really got to go."

"Does Steve have it?" she persisted.

"Please listen. I'm telling you what I told the others. I know nothing about Jack Ryder."

"Well," said Sandra, "maybe you could ask a few questions—"

"But there's nothing I want to find out," I replied, then turned away, ending the conversation and herding the kids toward the bus. On the way I slipped my hand around the shoulders of one of my three begonia bandits, turning her little face up to mine. "Noelle, sweetheart, you need to breathe. Take the flower stems out of your nose."

The first-graders and I arrived back at camp ten minutes late. The second-graders were waiting for me, bounding with energy. We walked and pranced and danced to the playing field.

"Okay, we're bunnies," I shouted, and everyone hopped.

"Okay, we're deer, use long legs, long legs. . . ."

The kids raced.

"Now, we're chickens. Peck, peck, peck, run, run on your little stick feet! Uh-oh, watch out, here comes the fox!"

That's how we passed beneath the shady hillside on which Jack and his class sat—a flock of little chickens and a loping, lip-smacking, red-haired fox.

"Hey," shouted Terry, "we're the foxes, you're the chicken."

"Okay. Peck, peck!"

They attacked me from all sides.

Lying on the grass, with a pile of laughing foxes collapsed around me, I looked up at the shimmering field of sky, then turned my head toward the hill on the right. The Wild Bunch, Eugene and his third-grade mates, were spread out beneath the old trees, quietly working on their drawings. Classical music drifted down to us—string music, as if a large harp hung in the elms. Jack was kneeling and talking to two of the kids. April, the plump little girl who wore the zillion glittery barrettes, came up from behind and hugged him.

"Hi, Coachie," Eugene called to me softly.

Jack looked down the hill. I gazed back at him. I wasn't sure if the long, easy smile was for me or the little kids.

For a moment I wished I were a kid. I wished I was sitting up on that peaceful hill, listening to Jack's music, and discovering ways to color summer. But my little foxes were wriggling around me, and I had to get them off to the playing field.

At lunch that day, Anna, Jack, and I were off duty. We got some pizza from the cafeteria, then each of us staked out a corner in the office, claiming our favorite piece of worn furniture. Anna was reading a Tolstoy novel, Jack was thumbing through Harry's *National Geographic,* and I had the sports page spread out. Between box scores, I glanced up, studying Jack. I had a strong hunch that the party girls and their questions weren't going to let up. And if I decided to slip Jack into Heather's lineup, maybe some information would help.

"Listen, Jack," I began, "there are some things I need to know about you."

He met my eyes and smiled. "Yeah? What?"

"Which do you prefer, blondes or brunets?"

The smile disappeared. "Excuse me?"

45

"Which do you prefer, girls with blond or dark hair."

"I know what 'brunets' means," he replied stiffly.

Anna glanced up from her book.

"So which is it?" I insisted.

"Aren't redheads a choice?" he asked.

"No," I said. "There weren't any redheads at last night's party."

He looked at me funny.

"At least none that I know of who are interested in you. So which is it?"

"I don't know," he mumbled. "It doesn't really matter."

"Oh, come on," I challenged him, "don't be one of those guys who claims that looks don't matter to you. I hate it when guys say that."

Anna closed her book, marking her place with a napkin. Jack looked from her to me. "Of course looks matter," he said defensively. "I'd be the first to tell you that. I just can't tell you exactly what look it is. When I see it, I know it."

"Short or tall?" I asked.

Jack sighed. "I draw the line at six-foot-five."

"Really? You'd go out with a girl five inches taller than you?"

"Four," he corrected me.

Six-foot-one, I noted mentally and took a quick bite out of my pizza. "Okay. Family background. Father, mother, sisters, brothers, pets? And what do they do?"

"My mother is an M.D. at Greater Baltimore Medical. Period," he said. He sounded annoyed. I wondered if family was a touchy subject.

46

"That's great," I said softly, encouragingly. "Just one question more. Well, more like two, part A and—"

"You know, Carly," he interrupted, "this kind of stuff usually comes out gradually as two people get to be friends."

"What's that supposed to mean?" I asked.

He shook his head. "Never mind."

"Did you leave a girlfriend up in Pennsylvania?"

"Who does it matter to?" he replied testily.

"Well, okay, let's skip to part B," I said quickly. "Are you looking around for someone new?"

"Tell me, does it matter to you? If it doesn't, why are you asking?" His eyes were a dark, midnight blue. He was definitely angry.

As it happened, I was a little peeved too. "I'll tell you why! Because I spent last night, and this morning as well, with a bunch of gaga girls who wanted to know every last detail of your life. What did you think was going on at that party—did you think that I had just won the Miss Congeniality contest? Did you *really* think all those people wanted to be friends with *me?*"

I took a breath. I had no idea how angry I was till then.

"All they wanted to know about was you. You and Heather, Heather and you—" I could feel myself ready to explode "—you were the stars!"

Anna was watching us, her head cocked. Jack sat quietly. I knew he was trying to figure me out, and I didn't want him to.

"Never mind," I said, attempting to wave away the whole mess. "You're right. I shouldn't be so nosy."

He chewed thoughtfully for a minute. "Maybe,"

he said at last, "you've convinced *yourself* that Heather is a star. I overheard you talking to some guy last night. You went on and on about her. Maybe you shouldn't talk her up so much."

I hunched over my lunch.

"But I thought that was part of a plan," he went on. "I've been watching you work and I figured you were trying to get Heather hooked up with somebody else so she wouldn't be chasing Eggbeaters."

"His name is Luke," I muttered.

"You were trying to work it so you would have . . . Luke . . . to yourself. Am I right?" he asked.

If I had bent any lower over my pizza, I would have gotten pepperoni stuck on my nose. "You're right. Absolutely right. . . . Satisfied?"

He laughed—more like snorted—then got up and left.

"Hi, Carly! It's me, Heather. Quick message. Are you sure it's okay about Tim coming over today? (Nervous giggle.) We'll probably talk about you the whole time. Call me."

Beep.

"Hello, Carly. Steve here. It's Saturday morning. I wanted to ask you about Heather."

Beep.

"Carly. It's Tim. Saturday. Eleven o'clock. Can we talk?"

Beep.

"Uh, is this Carly? This is Brent Coughlin. I met you at Steve's party. Could you call me back? 555-4639. But don't tell Steve I called, okay?"

Beep.

48

"Hi. This is Jill. I was at Steve's party. I *have* to talk to you, Carly. 555-J-I-L-L."

Beep.

"Carly. Tim again. Eleven-thirty. I've been thinking. I think . . . we should be just friends."

Beep.

"Hello. This message is for Carly, the friend of Jack. My name is Meredith. Please call me at 555-6280. Thank you."

Beep.

"No," I said to the whirring answering machine. "Thank *you*. Thank you all!" I threw down my message pad.

"Carly, this is Luke. I know this is kind of last minute, but I was wondering, would you go out with me tonight?"

But that message wasn't on the tape.

"What are you muttering?" Joelle asked as I pushed the machine's delete button.

"An ancient curse on sisters," I replied.

She smirked, then plopped a huge canvas bag on her bed. "Well, I guess *that's* easier to believe than your offer to drive me downtown to my doctor's appointment."

"Give me a break. I was being nice for a change."

"Or you were avoiding some phone calls," Joelle observed as she pulled the books out of her bag.

My sister has been carrying oversized purses stuffed with books since we were little kids. But now all the titles contained the word "baby." I missed the old, mysterious volumes on early societies and exotic cultures, in which, as a kid, I really had hunted for curses on older sisters.

"Why aren't you swimming at Heather's house?" Joelle asked.

I started folding laundry, not all of it clean. "She's having someone else over."

"Your boyfriend, Carly! Or at least, he was."

I gave up folding, opened various drawers, and tossed the stuff in. "Tim and I, we weren't meant for each other."

"Nor were you and any of the others," Joelle observed. "They were all meant for Heather."

I threw her clean purple bra at her. "No big loss. Look where love got you."

She blinked, and for a moment said nothing. Then she rose and padded over to her bureau, which was next to mine. Twin beds, twin bureaus. "I just don't get it, Carly. You're a fighter—in sports, in school, at home. But when it comes to Heather—" She shook her head. "It bothers me. I can't stand watching one person push around another. I can't stand watching my own sister get used."

I slammed shut all my drawers. "Then get a life, Joelle," I suggested, "and you won't have to waste your time watching mine."

SIX

THE FIRST THING I did Saturday afternoon was get Jack's telephone number from Directory Information. I then gave it to Meredith and 555-J-I-L-L, as well as the three other girls who called me that weekend. They each got the same piece of advice: "Jack's kind of an up-front and direct guy. You should call him yourself and ask all the questions you want. Don't be shy. Jack loves to answer questions about himself."

It took a little more time to deal with the Heather calls. I chatted up the guys some more and took notes so I could figure out the best order in which to line them up. I told them that she was dating somebody now, but I didn't think it would last long—which was true. I gave her and Tim a week before she decided she wasn't really interested.

During the weekend I waited, I hoped, I even prayed once, but I didn't hear a word from Luke. Of course, I wasn't sure that he even remembered my last name. After the day of the food fight, the gymnastics team started coming later to lunch—maybe on purpose—so I didn't get to talk to him. I was giving him one more day to casually bump into me before I used up my one excuse to make contact, the return of his towel. Hoping that Monday was my lucky day, I put on lipstick that morning and took the long route to Kirbysmith, entering at the college's main gate. To reach the student center, I had to ride past the gym.

I was rubbernecking, looking back over my shoulder to see who was getting out of the cars in the gym lot, when I suddenly lurched forward. My bike bolted up a curb. I squeezed the hand brakes hard and shrieked to a stop, face-to-face, wheel-to-metal with a huge garbage Dumpster. Slowly I let out my breath. Hoping no one had seen me, I backed up.

"You okay, Carly?"

I whirled around. Jack. Of course.

"That Dumpster ought to watch where he's going," Jack said. He kept a straight face, but the slight tremble in his voice gave away his laughter.

I pedaled slowly over to him, because if I raced off the way I wanted to, it would only look worse. "How was your weekend?" I asked politely.

"Okay," he said just as politely. "How about yours? Do anything exciting?"

"Yeah. Spent a lot of time on the phone." I glanced sideways at him.

"Me too," he said, his eyes sliding over to meet mine. But I would never admit that I had sicked all those panting girls on him.

I reluctantly got off my bike, dismounting awkwardly on the right side, and walked the bike between us.

"Listen, Carly—" Jack lifted his hand, and for a

moment I thought he was going to lay it on top of mine. Then he rested it on another part of the handlebars, walking the bike with me. "I'm sorry about Friday afternoon. I'm sorry for what I said about you and Heather and Eggbeaters—it's none of my business."

I nodded. I wasn't mad anymore. "That's okay. I'm sorry too."

"For what?" he asked. It sounded like a sincere question.

"For continuing to ask stuff when you made it obvious you didn't want to answer."

"Oh," he said. "I thought it was for giving all those girls my phone number and telling them how much I love questions about myself."

My mouth opened a little.

He laughed. This time one finger did graze mine, then he held out his hand. "Friends?"

I was a little surprised. I didn't think whether we got along mattered one way or the other to him. "Sure. Friends." I shook his hand. The bike went clattering down between us. We tried to catch it at the same time and knocked heads—that is, we knocked my hard helmet and Jack's head.

"Oh! Sorry!" I reached out to rub his forehead. As soon as I realized what I was doing, I pulled back self-consciously. But I had gotten close enough to smell him. That same good smell. "What kind of soap do you use?"

He handed me my bike. "Excuse me?"

"Never mind," I said quickly.

Great. We had just become friends, and I started right off with a personal question.

Jack squinted at me, then glanced over my shoulder. "Probably the same kind of soap he uses," he said sarcastically. "Macho Spring."

"Macho Spring?" I turned to see who Jack was eyeing.

It *was* my lucky day! Luke was jogging in a small circle in front of the gym. He looked as if he had just come back from a run, his whole body glistening in the sun. He saw us. I kept telling myself I was imagining things, but I was so sure his eyes lit up. Sea green eyes. Sea green eyes with streaks of golden sunlight in his hair. He trotted over.

"Carly." His voice sounded soft and husky. Maybe he was just out of breath. I sure was.

"Hi. Hi," I said. I caught myself before I repeated it for a third time. Every other word in the English language had deserted me.

"Hello," Jack said. "I'm Jack Ryder."

"Oh. Right. Sorry," I apologized. "Jack, this is Egg—" Beaters, I was about to say, because to Jack, that's who he was.

"Luke," Luke said quietly, as if I had forgotten his name.

"*Luke,*" I repeated too loudly. "I knew that!"

Jack laughed. "Looks like you've been working out," he said to Luke.

"I ran a few miles," Luke replied with a shrug. "Coach said he was going to work us hard today." He turned to me. "How are you, Carly?"

"Great."

"Me too. How's camp?"

"I love it. The kids are a challenge but really fun." I was flying now—I had managed two complete sentences. "Luke's a counselor there too," I said.

54

"Jack," Jack corrected me. "That's Luke. I'm Jack. You're Carly."

I flicked a glance at him and he laughed.

"Are you learning a lot from your new coach?" I asked Luke.

"Am I!" he said, his eyes fixed on me like two bright suns. "I'm learning that I'm the best. I just have to want it, Carly. I've got what it takes. I'm the best and can be even better. It's all mine, if I just want it enough."

"How long has self-confidence been a problem for you?" Jack asked deadpan.

I shot him another look. He pretended not to notice.

"Gee, I don't know," Luke replied. "I mean, I always thought I was better than the rest." He moved his arm. His muscles couldn't help but flex. "But I guess there was this little part of me that wasn't really sure about it."

I nodded encouragingly. "A good coach gives you the confidence to let you be all you can be."

Luke gripped my upper arm. "I knew you'd understand," he said with such heat and intensity, I could have melted like a taper in his hand. "I mean, you're kind of an athlete."

"She *is* an athlete," Jack said quietly.

"Carly, are you, uh, staying around later on?" Luke asked.

"Staying around?" I repeated, my heart giving a little skip.

"I didn't know if you had to work late or anything. There's a movie tonight on campus. I thought maybe if you were going to be around . . ." He seemed so shy all the sudden.

55

"What a coincidence!" I said. "We've got a meeting that will run late today."

"We do?" Jack asked with surprise.

I let my bike fall against him.

"Ow! That was subtle," he complained.

But Luke hadn't noticed. He was already edging away. "Well, if you want to meet me at the student center, uh—six o'clock?"

"Six o'clock," I called back to him.

I could hardly believe it. I walked along the road in a daze, letting Jack steer the bike. "Six o'clock," I sighed to myself. I was dying to tell Heather. I wanted to whoop and celebrate with my best friend Heather. But of course, the last person I could tell was my old friend Heather.

I turned to Jack. "Slap me five!"

Instead, he yanked me back from the path of an oncoming car.

Mondays I taught double sessions at the pool, working with the second-graders first, then Hau and his ESL kids. Hau and I described our style of team teaching as "doing opera." There was constant dialogue between us, me singing out instructions in English, him quickly filling in words—often squeezing in whole sentences in Vietnamese—both of us communicating with melodramatic arm gestures. The kids' heads would swing back and forth between us like an audience at a very fast opera.

But the show slowed down that morning at the pool. I couldn't keep my mind on my work, and Hau had to supply some English words as well. In class, Hau usually did whatever I did, so when I was doing my on-land demonstration of the crawl stroke, walking back and forth and telling the kids to watch my arms, he did the same. Then my best little fish, Tam, asked me if I could swim on my back.

"Sure, the backstroke is fun. I'll show you how it looks." Unfortunately I didn't think to look behind me. I wheeled my arms and walked backward, landing in the pool, rear first, arms and legs flailing.

Hau didn't miss a beat. Windmilling his arms, he walked backward and fell in next to me. The kids burst out laughing. Then they all wanted to try it.

I was still walking on air when the counselors gathered late that afternoon in the camp office.

"So," Jack said, "another inspiring class with athletics leader, Miss Carly."

He had been working with Hau's kids on cartoons, getting them to use both art and language. Anna was looking over the work to see what the kids had written. I barely glanced at the wet, wrinkled papers, but even from a distance I could see lots of splashes of red hair and blue pools and wavy arms.

"I'm surprised you haven't encouraged them to write songs about me too," I said to Jack.

"Oh, they don't need any encouraging," he replied.

"How'd your day go?" Harry asked me. His freckled hands rested easily on his desk; his face was smiling, gentle as a big, friendly dog's, but he was watching me.

"Fine," I said. "Why are you asking?"

He shrugged and smiled. "No real reason. You seemed a little out of it. Oh, I'm not complaining,

Carly," he added in response to my frown. "Just curious. You called me Larry at lunch today."

I gave him an apologetic smile.

"Twice."

"Oh."

"Larry. That's Harry with an *L* for Luke," Jack said.

I guess he thought he was clever, coming up with that theory.

"Luke's an Olympic hero who asked her to a campus movie tonight," he went on. "Does that explain a few things today?"

"Did he ask you, really?" Pamela gushed. Playtime had again taken a toll on her pink frost fingertips. She was gluing on a long plastic nail that was sharp enough to slice tomatoes. "Awesome!"

"That's what I think," I said, rising from my seat. "I'd better get going now. I've got to put on some clean clothes." I figured I had just enough time to get myself halfway to awesome.

"But you're working late," Jack reminded me. "That's what you told him. Won't he notice if you change?"

I looked at Jack as if he were utterly stupid. "I'm going to wash and dry these and put them back on."

He looked at me as if I were utterly crazy. "Is it worth it?"

"Luke's a lucky guy," Hau said kindly. "Have a good time, Carly."

"I will. Thanks," I said and rushed out the door.

Of course, I took the back route out of the college. I didn't want to run into Luke or Heather, whose dance studio was right next to the gym. As I pedaled

58

home, I entertained myself by explaining to Heather why I hadn't told her about Luke and me, even though we had been dating for three hot and heavy months. It was a wonderful fantasy and I explained to her over and over in great detail.

Imagine then, how confused I was when I found in the middle of one explanation that I really was looking at Heather's face. It was at an intersection close to my house and she was stretching across the front seat of her Honda.

"Carly, I've been following you for five blocks!"

I knew it was preposterous, but I got this crazy, really paranoid idea that Heather had tagged me with an invisible beeper and whenever I made contact with a good-looking guy, it sent signals to her. Somehow, she knew.

"They told me at the camp office about your terrific news," she said.

"They—who? Jack?" And he said we were friends. Traitor!

"No," Heather replied. "The Vietnamese guy and the girl with the nails. Jack was kind of quiet."

"Oh." *Sorry, Jack,* I thought.

Cars started beeping. The light had changed.

I pedaled on to the next intersection. Heather put on her yellow blinkers and trailed me.

"I'm really happy for you, Carly," she said when we had stopped again.

I leaned forward on my handlebars so I could see her face clearly in the car. Looking back at me were the same big gray eyes that had wished me luck before basketball games and job interviews and math tests. I was acting like an idiot. How had I gotten so jealous and weird? "Thanks," I said softly. "I needed to hear that."

"I really am so happy for you! I wish it had worked out for me and Tim the way it's working out for you guys."

So, she and Tim had already bombed. She was happy for me all right. My date with Luke meant she was one step closer to *her* date with Luke.

I tried to squelch a toad-pool of ugly thoughts as we rode the next two blocks. Heather stopped in front of my house. I put down my kickstand and walked around to the driver's side of the car.

"I'm sorry about Tim," I said, "but I've got good news for you. Half the guys at the party the other night fell for you."

"Yeah?"

I was glad to see the pink cheeks. "Yeah, yeah! Steve for one."

"Oh, Steve," she said.

"What's wrong with Steve?" I demanded. "He's cute. He's nice. He's got money. And his own car."

She shrugged him off.

"Okay, how about Brent?"

She frowned. "Brent . . ."

"Tall, dark, soulful eyes. Said he had an entire room dedicated to his rock music collection. Gets tickets to all the concerts and—"

She shook her head.

"All right. How about André? Blond. Father has a skybox at Camden Yards. I think he sails a lot."

"You know I get seasick, Carly."

"Well, there are others who called me, but if you're going to be that picky . . ." I chided her.

"I'm not being picky," she whined. "But the guys at Steve's party, they just hang out. I don't care if

60

they're rich—I can pay their way. I want a guy who really does something."

Like gymnastics, I thought.

"I want a guy who cares about something and can talk about something. One who doesn't just hang out and fool around all day."

The wheels started turning in my head. Jack didn't hang out. He worked and he cared about kids. He loved art and music like she did, and he was a good talker.

Jack would help me out. I mean, we were friends, weren't we? And even though we were just friends, I knew he had a great bod and thick hair that any girl would like to get her hands into. And his eyes, that intense and moody blue . . .

"Carly? What are you thinking?"

I blinked his picture out of my mind before I got carried away.

"I've got to think some more," I said, but I knew already: Jack was it, first guy in line, the perfect match.

"Think about what?" Heather asked, frustrated.

"Someone who could be *true love* at last," I told her. "Listen, Heather, I've got to run."

"But—"

"I'm meeting Luke at six, and I'm a long way off from awesome."

As I ran my bike up the driveway I heard her call out, "I'm really, really happy for you."

SEVEN

"ALL I'M ASKING for is a ride back to campus," I said to my sister an hour and a half later. "What else did you have planned for tonight? Reading chapter two on Buddy's toilet training?"

"All I'm saying is drive yourself," Joelle replied, plunking down a plate on the kitchen table. "Why do you need a chauffeur?"

"We have two cars, Kitten," my father interjected.

I hated it when he called me that. The nickname hadn't suited me even when I was four.

"Your mother is going to sigh all night over her students' hopeless essays," he continued, patting his reddish hair, an unconscious habit that developed after he started combing it in odd ways to hide the thin spots. "And I'm preparing for the lit conference. Both cars are free."

"Oh, never mind," I huffed, pushing back my chair. How could I explain?

I was supposed to be on campus already. Luke knew from this morning that I had ridden my bike. After the movie, I planned to tell him that I'd left it in the camp office but didn't want to bike home in the dark. Then I'd ask for a ride. That way, if we didn't exchange phone numbers, he'd at least know where I lived. But if I told the plan to Joelle, and things didn't work out with Luke, it would be one more guy she'd needle me about.

I hurried upstairs and put on some mascara and peach-colored lipstick, though I'd probably lick off most of Cinnamon Sunset by the time I got there. At least my hair was neatly rebraided and I no longer wore Eugene's sticky hand prints on my stomach.

I was wheeling my bike out of the garage when Joelle strolled outside, holding up the car keys, jingling them. "I'll take you if you tell me why."

I put away the bike and rode with her to Kirbysmith in silence. "Right here's fine," I said, when we had reached the edge of campus, then I climbed out quickly.

"Aren't you going to tell me why?" my sister called to my back.

"I'll tell you . . . after you tell me the reason you suddenly went soft and offered me a ride," I replied, and closed the door. "You can't be that curious, Joelle," I said through the window. "And you've never been that nice. Must be raging mother hormones."

"Brat." She roared off.

Luke was waiting for me outside the student center, sitting on an elevated block of sunny concrete that flanked the steps. One leg was straight out, the other drawn up, a muscular arm resting lightly on his bare knee. He could have been a piece of sculpture, some Olympic god gracing the student temple. His eyes were closed so he didn't see me staring at him.

"Luke . . . Luke?" I said a little louder.

"Oh. Carly."

"Hard day?" I asked softly.

He smiled. His eyes made me think of hazy green summer.

"You bet. A double-strength workout. When you're at the top, coaches are tough on you." He leaped down beside me. "Some friends of mine are saving us a seat inside."

The small auditorium was only half-filled. I guess *Volcano Warriors* wasn't a big draw. A professor, who looked as if he had been caught in the same fashion time warp as my mother, gave the audience, which was mostly his film class, a lecture on B-grade sci-fi flicks. He went on and on about all the stuff of the unconscious that we were about to see come pouring out of this volcano.

I sat between Luke and two guys named Hank and Josh, gymnastic teammates who attended Kirbysmith. Though my eyes were on the lecturer, I was sharply aware of every move Luke made. His arm bumped mine. His thumb twitched. He yawned.

"You interested in films?" Hank asked me, loud enough to disturb the students who were trying to hear the lecture.

"Or Luke?" Josh said, grinning at me.

"Actually, I love sports," I replied quietly. "But films are fun."

"Do you love sports heroes?" Josh asked, still grinning. With his big head, he reminded me of a jack-o'-lantern.

"Do you consider yourself one?" I asked back.

Hank, who was dark-haired and probably thought

himself nice-looking, turned and laughed in Josh's face.

"Carly's kind of an athlete," Luke said.

She is an athlete, I heard Jack say in my mind.

"Really," said Hank. "What do you play?"

"Field hockey, basketball, and lacrosse for school. Softball for a recreation team."

"Are your teams any good?" asked Hank.

"No, we stink," I felt like saying, but he was Luke's friend.

"Ask Luke," I said proudly. After all, the girls had been state champs in basketball and lacrosse. "They're his school teams too."

Luke looked blank. "I, uh, don't really follow them. The guys' basketball team is pretty good."

The guys, for your information, have won four games in the last three years.

"You should have seen the girls from the college gymnastics team stopping to watch today," big-faced Josh told me. "Luke gave them a real performance. I thought the girls would never leave."

Who was this guy, Luke's agent?

"Oh, I've heard about the women's team," I said. "Too bad you guys couldn't go to the regionals with them."

I glanced sideways at Luke, but the put-down seemed to go right over his head. It didn't go over the heads of the other guys, however; Hank gave me a sly look. Josh changed the subject to athletic injuries.

The three guys discussed their injuries and treatments with the same enthusiasm and detail as my mother discussed childbirth experiences with Joelle. I found myself staring at parts of Luke's body as he described one problem, then the next. He seemed reluctant to end the conversation even when the movie had started. After several loud shushes from people around us, we settled down to watch things coming out of a volcano that looked to me not like dark forms of the unconscious but messed up Jell-O molds. They didn't look like anything to Luke: he slept through the last half.

When the lights came on, I gave him a little shake.

"Want to get something to drink?" Hank asked as we filed out of the auditorium. "Want to hang with us at the dorm lounge?"

"Or are you two ready to start making out?" Josh said, his pumpkin face gleaming.

"I could use a cold soda," I replied, refusing to take the bait.

Luke nodded agreeably. I'm not sure he even saw the bait dangling in front of him.

The lounge was on the second floor of a coed dorm. It was a big, carpeted room with lots of square cushion chairs gathered into groups. Tabletops were covered with crumbs and sticky stuff, and a microwave looked as if bombs of tomato sauce had been exploded in it. A girl sat in one corner, wired to her CD player, typing on a laptop. She glanced at us, then went back to her work.

I guess I should have been thrilled to be one girl sitting with three hunky guys in a college lounge, but I was quickly growing bored with story after story of athletic injuries and incredible feats on high bars and horses. When Josh suddenly got up and walked out, I turned to Luke, hopeful we could leave too.

He smiled back at me, looking into my eyes, and

said, "And then there was the Junior Invitationals, when I was eight. . . ."

A few minutes later Josh returned with a cooler. He grinned at us and opened it. Beer. Lots of it. No wonder Kirbysmith's men didn't make it to the regionals.

He pulled out two cans and offered them to us.

"No thanks. I never drink," Luke told him.

But a cold one was put in his hand anyway, and another put in mine. When I didn't open it, Hank leaned across a table and flipped open the top. I set it down with a thump. Luke held onto his and took a small, careful sip. Then another.

Hank and Josh drank in big gulps. I figured they were the kind who took pride in their burps.

"So you think Coach Milani's men have a chance against us?" Hank asked, settling back in his chair.

"You mean Milani's *boys?*" Luke responded, taking a sip from his can.

"You mean Milani's *girls!*" Josh said.

The three of them roared with laughter. The joke didn't seem that funny to me. They talked on and on about people in gymnastics, gossiping worse than girls. Sip by sip, Luke drank his beer.

When he was finished, he said, "I gotta go."

I got up, thinking he meant we were leaving. But Josh pointed Luke toward the men's room.

When Luke emerged, I was standing by the door of the lounge. "Sorry, I have to work tomorrow," I told him.

Luke nodded and headed back toward the chairs where Josh and Hank were still sitting. *So, I'm leaving alone,* I thought. Then he picked up my beer, waved to his friends with it, and followed me out.

"I need fresh air," he said, leaning on me as we made our way to the dorm elevator. I walked as straight as I could. It was hard to believe that Luke Hartly was that close to me, touching me, relying on me. Of course, old ladies have done the same when I've helped them search for their cars at the mall.

When we were outside again, the cool night air seemed to revive him. "Would you like to walk a little, Carly?" he said in that deep, soft voice of his.

"Yeah," I almost whispered.

We walked in silence for a few minutes, then I began telling him about the camp kids, the devilish Eugene, and Tam, who loved the water, and Miguel, my natural athlete.

"He's got a ton of talent for a little second-grader, but he needs lots of encouragement," I said. "All the counselors are trying to—"

"I needed a lot of encouragement when I was in second grade," Luke said. "I still do."

"Miguel's problem may be bigger than doing well in sports," I told him. "We think he's been abused at home."

"The coach I'm with now, he thinks abuse is encouragement," Luke said. "I've never been pushed so hard." He took several thirsty gulps of the beer. Then he went on to talk about what we had been talking about all night—*him*.

We walked a worn path that led to the stream with the wooden bridge. When we entered the grove of trees, he grew silent.

"You like it here, don't you?" I asked quietly.

He smiled. "It's nice being with you, Carly," he replied. "It's nice talking to you."

We sat down on the bridge, dangling our feet over the side, our toes just touching the water, resting our arms and chins on the lower plank of the railing. Moonlight splashed down through the trees and ran silvery patterns in the stream.

Luke drank some more of my beer. "So camp's fun," he said.

"Yeah, but sad too, in some ways," I replied. "Kids like Miguel and Eugene had never swum in a pool before. April thinks the green hills of a golf course are the most beautiful things she's ever seen."

Luke listened quietly. I knew, I just knew that if I got him away from those two macho jocks, everything would be different. I told him about other kids. He listened so intently, he didn't move. Then I realized he was asleep.

"Luke. Luke? Luke!"

He mumbled something.

"Wake up, Luke!"

He raised his head, smiled at me angelically, then laid his cheek back down on his arm, closing his eyes.

I picked up his beer can. Empty. I figured he was worn out from a tough day in the gym, dehydrated, and probably telling the truth when he said he never drank. There wasn't much I could do but wait it out. I glanced at my watch. 9:30. When I glanced at it again, it was 9:45. 9:55. 10:05. What if he took all night to sleep it off?

"Luke!"

"Mmm," he said, smiling.

I couldn't leave him there all night. I imagined him slipping under the bridge railing. I could see the headlines of tomorrow's paper: Olympic God

Found Dead In Stream. Camp Counselor Sought.

"Come on, Luke, come on," I begged. "Eggbeaters!" I shouted into his ear. I stood and pulled his arms up. His chin thumped down on the railing. I pulled and tugged and dragged, determined to get him off the bridge. By the time I had him safely sprawled on the bank, I was drenched with sweat. Hoping no one else was out for a moonlight stroll by the stream, I rolled him from one side to the other, searching his pockets.

Wallet, quarters, chewing gum—no keys. I thought about my choices. Campus Security. The Hank & Josh show. Joelle.

I didn't want to get Luke into trouble at the college. And Hank and Josh couldn't be trusted. There was no other alternative. I raced to the nearest dorm and made the call from a first-floor pay phone.

Twenty minutes later, wearing rubber flip-flops and a baggy undershirt that belonged to Dad, Joelle stood with her head cocked, staring down at Luke.

He had started mumbling, which was a hopeful sign; we might be able to get him to his feet.

"You sure know how to pick 'em," she said, shaking her head.

"Well, you've got to admit he's great looking."

"You should have called Heather," Joelle told me. "Let her have him *now*."

I bit my lip.

"She's been calling you—left two messages on the answering machine. She's *really, really* happy for you."

"Just help me get him home," I hissed.

"Okay, Sleeping Beauty," Joelle said, lifting up one of Luke's arms. "The pregnant lady's here to help."

We dragged him up to a sitting position, continually shouting at him. He blinked at us as if he had been under a spell for a hundred years. We each got under an arm and, struggling and grunting like two weight lifters, pulled ourselves up into a standing position. Then the three of us staggered down the path.

Joelle ended up driving the car over the campus lawn to get it closer. If we had been caught, two daughters of the chairperson of the English department, we would have had to find a new home. But security was lax that night. We shoved Luke into the backseat and took off.

EIGHT

IT WAS TEMPTING to leave him on his front steps, ring the doorbell, and run. But by the time I got Luke up to the porch, he was gazing at me adoringly and trying to apologize. His mother answered the door. Her arms were the same size as his, and her voice an octave lower than mine. In times like this, I knew that honesty was the only policy. I hoped that tomorrow, when Luke's head cleared, he would still be looking at me with those sweet, green, grateful eyes.

Joelle and I arrived home well after eleven.

"Dad and I were starting to worry," my mother said, glancing up from a pile of student papers. "It's late for a Monday night."

"Well, I was hoping a friend would give me a ride," I explained, "but he wasn't feeling good, so Joelle and I ended up taking him home instead."

Mom nodded understandingly. "I knew I could count on you two to take care of each other," she said and went back to her work. That's how it is when your parents are former sixties peace-and-love activists who went into education and had children late in their careers. Lucky for them, Joelle and I didn't turn out to be juvenile delinquents.

We trudged upstairs, and Joelle headed straight for the bathroom. Stretching out on my bed, I hypnotized myself by watching the blinking light on the answering machine. If I'd been smart, I'd have played the messages while Joelle had the water blasting. But at least two of the five blinks were Heather's, and I just couldn't stand to hear how really, really happy she was for me.

"Aren't you going to check your messages?" Joelle asked when she returned to the room, her short hair waving around her face like damp red feathers.

"It's late," I replied, "too late to call back. Why bother with it now?"

"It's like a soap opera. I'd think you'd want to catch up."

I shrugged, pulled the ponytail holder out of my hair, and began to unbraid it.

"Heather is really, really—" she began.

"I know," I cut my sister short.

"But Tim is wondering why he hasn't heard from Heather."

"Well, take a hint, Tim," I said.

Joelle's fingers hovered over her tray of lotions and vitamins. "In message three, Heather is really—"

"I *know!*"

"—being driven crazy by Tim's calls."

"Serves her right," I grumbled.

"And of course, she's really you-know-what," my sister added, choosing a large bottle of apricot cream stuff. "Steve, meanwhile, is kind of confused about

73

Heather. He says she blows hot and warm. I think he means hot and cold."

"Good luck, Steve," I said, yanking out the last twist of hair.

"Then there's 555-JILL," Joelle went on.

I rolled my eyes.

"Who is this Jack guy?"

"A friend, sort of. Someone I work with."

"He showed up in another message too. That girl left her E-mail address." Joelle rubbed the lotion down her pale freckled legs. Every night she examined them for varicose veins. "Carly, why have you suddenly become a dating hot line?"

"It's just one of those things," I said.

"Nothing that's ever happened to you has been 'just one of those things.' You're up to something."

I ran a big-toothed comb through my rippling hair.

"I think it has to do with Sleeping Beauty," Joelle said. "Would you like to hear my theory?"

"No."

"You've got the hots for the Sleeping B. That's obvious. And you actually think you can keep Heather away from him," she said, shaking her head with disbelief.

When I didn't react, she went on. "Tim thinks he dumped you, but you dumped him first, hoping to keep Heather occupied."

"Nobody dumped anybody," I said crisply. "It was by mutual agreement."

She dismissed the point with a wave of her lotion bottle. "All these other guys, you've somehow got them lined up for Heather. Only this time," she added with a sarcastic little smile, "I don't think you're planning to date them first."

I bit my lip.

"Am I right?"

"If you say so."

"What I can't figure out is how Jack and these other girls fit in," Joelle added.

"The other girls don't. But Jack, he could be the perfect guy."

"Carly, come on, you can't really think this scheme is going to work."

"What I think is that Heather just has to find the right guy. And I'm helping her do that."

"Oh pul-lease!" Joelle began plumping the zillion pillows that are on her bed. She'd always had a few; now she had a zillion, a collection of shapeless stuffed animals to comfort her. "The perfect guy for Heather is whatever guy you're dating. You should have figured that out long ago. I don't know why you dumped Tim—you should have ditched Heather."

"She's my friend," I said between clenched jaws.

"She's using you, Carly! Shy, sweet little Heather is using you. You call that friendship? I call it pathetic. Heather is a very selfish person. And if you think that by playing the fool you're being a loyal friend, well, I feel sorry for you."

"Playing the fool? You should know a thing or two about that, shouldn't you, Joelle?" I said, picking up one of her pillows and punching it. "I sure hope Sam appreciates it."

Joelle blinked. She had never told us the name of the baby's father.

"Next time, put away your own laundry," I told

her. "I saw his name on the back of a photo in your sock drawer. He looks old."

"He is a little older," Joelle replied quietly. "He's a graduate student in anthropology, a TA."

"A teaching assistant?" I exclaimed. "You mean he taught you? Oh, man," I said, disgusted. "I hope he gave you at least a *B. B* for baby."

Joelle folded back the sheet on her bed and carefully arranged her pillows. That's how she always responded to things she didn't want to deal with. She'd busy herself, retreating to her own world. She could close her eyes and close me right out.

"Joelle," I said while I had the chance. "Buddy is Sam's baby too. He should help out. Sam should help you through."

She clicked off the light above her bed. "He can't."

"Well," I said smugly, glad to throw her words back in her face, "I call *that* pathetic. Sam is a very selfish person."

"He's married."

For a moment I stood dumbfounded. "Married?"

My sister and an older, married man? What had happened to the model student who had gone off to college with big dreams of studying the peoples of West Africa? How had she turned into a stay-at-home, unwed mother in suburban Baltimore? "And you criticize Heather for stealing boyfriends. Cripe, you went after somebody's husband!"

"I didn't know—not at first," Joelle replied, her voice half-smothered by a pillow.

"But you found out."

"Too late," she said. "I was already in love with him . . . so in love with him." She lifted her head up for a moment, speaking in a clear voice. "Still am."

I shook my head. "And what about him?"

"He's married," she said flatly, then dropped her head.

"That's why you're always hanging around our phone, isn't it—you're waiting for him to call."

"He's called twice. I listened while he talked, then erased the messages."

I sucked in a deep breath and let it out slowly.

"Take your shower, Carly," Joelle said in a tired, dull voice. "It's getting late. We both need sleep. All three of us need sleep." She rested her hand on her stomach.

I turned off the lamp on my side and headed for the bathroom. When I returned to the room twenty minutes later, Joelle quickly turned her back to me, her eyes closed as if she were asleep. But in the shimmer of moonlight I had already seen her silent tears.

"Strike three!"

"Miguel, Miguel, couldn't hit a Taco Bell," a little voice chanted.

I turned around slowly, wearing my sternest umpire look, and surveyed a row of damp, smudgy faces. I had shown up for work Tuesday morning exhausted from a night of tossing and turning, thinking about Joelle. I wasn't in the mood for any grief from the second-graders. "Did someone say something?"

A row of innocent faces looked back at me from the bench. Miguel, blinking his eyes quickly, took his place at the end, leaving plenty of room between him and his teammates.

I had to be careful in what I said, careful not to humiliate Miguel further. Obviously, yesterday's little lecture on sportsmanship and the one I'd given last Friday on team play had had no effect.

"Someone spoke, and I want to know who."

Half the kids looked straight at me, the other half looked down at their feet.

"Okay," I said. "You all can take the field. You just gave away your last two outs."

Now the kids turned to look angrily at the one who had said it, but I knew she wasn't the only camper who had been razzing Miguel. It had been going on since last week, and it baffled me. Miguel looked as if he wanted to crawl under a rock.

I was glad when we had to stop the game for lunch. Jack, Anna, and I were off duty that day.

"I just don't get it," I said to them, pulling myself up to sit on a brick wall. They had found a place in the dappled shade of a campus oak tree and had brought my lunch and soda out for me.

"Miguel's my ace fielder," I went on, popping open a can. "Last week, he threw a ball to me harder and more accurately than any second-, third-, or fourth-grader I've ever known. So I figured there'd be a ton of opportunities to give him the praise he needs."

Anna nodded as she listened. Jack was looking at me, but I wasn't sure if he heard any of the words I was saying.

"Last Wednesday Miguel messed up on a play," I continued, "and messed up again right after that. One kid started getting on him, then another, and another. I understand that—everybody's glad to make some other kid the class turkey. What I don't get is why Miguel doesn't fight back."

"Fight back how?" Anna asked.

"Well, he's a natural athlete. I can see it in the way he moves," I told her. "I keep giving him chances to prove the others wrong, but he flubs up every time."

Anna nodded. Jack gazed down at his sandwich as if deep in thought. *Maybe I bore guys to death,* I thought. *In a moment, he'll be asleep like Luke.*

"I think Miguel is left-handed like me," Jack said quietly. "I'm pretty sure he paints with that hand. Could he be trying to do sports with his right?"

"I don't know," I replied thoughtfully. "But now that I think about it, he's the kind of kid who does exactly as you tell him. That could be it! I wonder if I could find him a little left-hander's glove. You could be right, Jack!" I exclaimed, shaking him by the arm so that the sandwich in his hand wavered by his mouth, losing some of its lettuce. "Oh. Sorry."

He smiled at me, then took a bite.

"I sure hope you're right," I went on. "I know we're not supposed to have favorites, but I really feel for this kid."

"Well, you can't help having favorites," Anna said. "The fact is kids are people. They have personalities, and we're all going to fall for certain kids the same way we fall for someone our own age. We just can't show it," she added.

The three of us chewed silently.

"It's funny, isn't it?" I said to Anna. "The way you fall for someone. Sometimes, it's bang, right away."

She nodded.

"But other times, it sneaks up on you. You suddenly realize you're thinking about this one person all the time. You're always waiting, always hoping to see that one person."

Anna glanced at Jack.

"Like Eggbeaters?" Jack suggested.

"Like Luke," I said stubbornly.

"So, how was last night?" he asked.

I knew he'd inquire sooner or later. "Fine."

"Fine?" Jack repeated. "After racing home, washing, drying, and ironing your clothes—ironing your hair too, I guess—all you can say is 'fine'?"

"Well, what do you want?" I asked angrily. "The blow-by-blow account?"

"Probably," said Anna, capping her water bottle.

"The movie was extremely interesting," I told them coolly.

Jack grinned. "Wasn't it the one where all the creatures look like weird Jell-O molds?"

"Yes," I said. "I'd think an artsy-fartsy type like you would really enjoy something like that."

"I didn't say I didn't. I was just curious to hear what you thought about it."

"It was fine," I replied, my jaw tight.

"I think we've established that the movie and date were fine," Anna said quietly.

"Anna and I were walking across campus this morning," Jack went on. "You know that grassy area by the woods and stream?"

"The Commons," I replied cautiously.

"You know that big sign for Kirbysmith College? Someone drove up on the grass last night—must have caught it with a fender and pulled the whole thing down."

"There's no way we hit that thing!" I burst out.

Jack and Anna looked at each other, then threw back their heads and laughed.

"Pay up, Anna," Jack said, "I told you those tire tracks were hers."

"Well, then you were wrong," I cut in. "My sister was driving."

"Your sister?" His blue eyes were bright with laughter. "You mean there's another one like you?"

"No, there is not. We couldn't be more different," I told him.

"You owe me, Jack," Anna said, laying her hand on his. It was a casual gesture, but I noticed it because Anna wasn't a touching type. She and Jack had gotten close in a short period of time.

Anna took her hand away and crumpled up her lunch bag. "Well, there's a stack of teaching texts waiting for me at the library," she said.

"Need help carrying them?" Jack asked, tossing her bag for her ten feet to the trash, landing a perfect shot.

"No, no," she said quickly, "finish your lunch. But thanks, Jack." She gave him a slow, beautiful smile.

Was there something between them? I wondered.

"She's nice," I said as Anna walked away.

"She really is," Jack agreed.

"Are you dating her?"

Jack choked on his sandwich. "Excuse me?"

"Are you dating her?"

"She's a senior in college," he reminded me. "We're friends, that's all."

"Oh. Like you and me."

He hesitated. "Sort of."

I swung my feet, kicking my heels against the brick wall. "Meaning you and I are just sort of friends?"

"Why are you asking?"

81

"Why are you always asking why I'm asking?" I asked.

We stared at each other nose-to-nose, then both of us turned away.

"Okay, here's how it is," I told him. "If you're a friend, I want to ask for a favor. Actually," I corrected myself, "let me put it this way. I'm about to do you a great favor. A fantastic favor. I have a terrific idea. Heather."

"Heather what?"

"Heather Larsson. How could you forget? I think you two would be a perfect match."

"You do?"

I saw how tightly he pressed his lips together. "You don't have to get nervous—"

"I'm not," he said, his mouth a tense line.

"Then sound excited," I told him. "There are a hundred guys who'd die for me to set them up with her. Heather is gorgeous. She's a sexy dresser. Her large gray eyes can turn a guy to putty. She—"

"Save it," Jack said. "I heard it all at Steve's party." He jumped off the wall and paced in front of me. "You know, Carly, you think you know a lot more about guys than you do. You think we're all the same and that we all like the same kind of girl. Maybe you think we're all stupid."

"But you don't know—"

"What's worse," he said, spinning around to face me, putting his hands on the wall on either side of me, moving in way too close, "you think you can manipulate us. You believe you've got me figured out. You think you can handle me like you handled the rest of them at the party, use me for your own purposes. I hate it. Hate it."

I swallowed hard and stared into his stormy blue eyes.

He backed off. "This sneaking around, trying to set up Heather and everybody—Heather and me—if you want Eggbeaters that badly, fight for him fair and square."

"But you don't know Heather. You don't know about Craig and Todd and Lenny and Taylor and Bo and Tim—oh, I can't remember them all—but I dated every one of them. Right before Heather did. I'm not kidding you," I added when he looked at me doubtfully. "She took them all. Ask my sister."

"Then why do you stay friends with her?"

"Because I'm a fool!" I exploded. "Isn't that obvious? I care about this person who cares about me, but cares about herself a whole lot more. I'm a stupid fool! Go ahead, feel sorry for me. My sister does. . . . But I guess Joelle and I have to feel sorry for each other," I added, biting my lip.

I don't know why I did it then. I don't cry easily and never do it around other people, but tears were stinging in my eyes. I was feeling totally miserable and confused about Heather. I was incredibly angry. But I knew my sister had been just as much of a sucker, and that my misery couldn't compare with hers. I couldn't begin to understand how bad Joelle felt.

"Carly," Jack said softly, and caught with his finger a big roller coming down my cheek. I squeezed shut my eyes, but my nose still ran. I dropped my head so strands of hair would fall and cover my face, then dug deep in my pockets. He gently brushed back the hair and handed me a tissue.

"Carly, listen to me," Jack said, bending down to see my face. "When you care a lot about another person, you're bound to do something that most people think is foolish."

"Sure. I bet you and Anna do all the time."

"I don't know about Anna, but I'm real good at it. Getting better every day," he added dryly.

"That's hard to believe," I said sniffling. "You're sort of a hunky cool type."

He grimaced. "Thank you . . . I think."

I smiled a little.

"Okay, how's this for an idea," Jack said. "I'll go out with Heather if you want me to, but only if you go too, and we make it a kind of casual group thing."

I considered the offer. "Actually, that would be better. Heather runs when a guy comes on too strong. It's better if she doesn't think she's being set up."

"She's not being set up," he said quickly. "Carly, you can't assume I'm interested in Heather. If it happened that I was, I wouldn't want your help. I wouldn't need it," he added confidently. "Let's just all go out and have a good time, okay?"

"Okay," I said brightly. But I knew how it would go, and later on that day, I asked Harry if he'd like to come with us to a carnival Thursday night. After all, three's a crowd. I wanted someone to talk to when Jack started gazing into Heather's beautiful eyes.

NINE

"SO THIS IS Jack," Joelle said on Thursday evening. My father had answered the door, exchanged a few polite words with Jack and Harry, then padded off to the den with his *Macworld* magazine. Naturally my sister felt compelled to make up for the lapse in parental cross-examination.

I had tried to reason with her earlier that evening. "It's not a real date, Joelle," I'd explained. "Not for me, so there's no need to check out the guys."

"Sorry, but I've been following this soap opera for a week and a half. I'm not missing a chance to meet one of the main characters."

Now she gave both guys a serious once-over. Harry blushed.

"I've heard a lot about you," Joelle said to Jack.

"Really?" he glanced at me, smiling, uncertain.

"Well, not from Carly, but you're a popular topic on our answering machine," Joelle told him.

"Oh. And you, you must be the one who laid

85

the tire tracks on Kirbysmith Commons," Jack said.

Joelle laughed. "So Carly told you about Sleeping Beauty."

"Sleeping Beauty?" Jack looked intrigued.

"Joelle," I said in a soft, warning voice.

"What a guy," Joelle said, shaking her head.

Jack turned to me, his eyes glittering. He must have guessed she was talking about Eggbeaters—Luke— whatever. I hadn't heard from Luke since Monday night and had ducked every attempt by Jack and the other counselors to find out how things had gone.

I turned to Harry, whom I was counting on to shepherd us along cheerfully, just as he did at work. But Harry had mysteriously changed into another person. Instead of clapping his hands and saying, "Okay, guys, let's go, and let's make this the best carnival ever!" he stood still on the exact spot where he had entered the living room.

"Joelle, this is Harry, our fearless leader," I said, hoping to snap him out of it.

Harry smiled, looking a little nervous. I waited for him to extend his hand the way he always did, making you feel as if you were shaking the paw of a friendly bear. But his hands dangled by his sides as if he were a guy at his first dance. "Nice to meet you, Joelle."

"Well, we don't want to keep Heather waiting," I said.

"Why not?" Joelle asked.

Jack laughed.

"Joelle," Harry said, "would you like to come along with us?"

My sister stared at him, then her cheeks flushed. It was the first color I had seen in her face since she had come home pregnant.

"Just what I need," she said tartly, "a bunch of rides to give me evening as well as morning sickness."

Harry looked at her puzzled.

"I guess Carly didn't tell you our little family secret. I've got a baby in here." She patted her stomach.

I wasn't sure if Harry's short hair really stood on end or if his reddening scalp just made it look that way. "Oh . . . well . . . that's wonderful. Congratulations!"

Joelle managed something between a grimace and a smile. Harry looked as if he wanted to escape through the nearest window. I gave him a light push toward the door.

"I'm sorry you can't come with us," Jack said. "I'd like to hear more about Sleeping Beauty."

"Oh, I could tell you lots of interesting things," Joelle replied and winked.

I yanked him through the door.

Harry remained quiet all the way to Heather's house. I sat in the front seat with Jack, giving him directions and a bit of romantic advice.

"Carly," he said at last, "I thought I told you, this is not a date. This is not a setup. It's just a group of people going out together."

"Right. And this is just a theoretical discussion. I'm telling you what I've observed about dating—and about Heather because I happen to know her best—in case some time in the future it might be useful to you."

He sighed.

"I mean, there are so many little opportunities for a guy—turn left. Left!" I shouted.

Jack pulled the wheel, and the car squealed around the corner. "Next time," he said, "tell me before we've crossed the intersection, okay?"

"For instance," I went on. "You and a girl are watching the sun set, or the moon rise, or harbor lights, whatever. Where do you stand?"

"What do you mean where?" Jack asked. "Is this a trick question?"

"Just tell me where."

"Give me a multiple choice," he said.

"A. In front of her. B. Beside her. C. Behind her."

He shrugged. "B. Beside her."

"Wrong."

"Well, maybe it's wrong for you," Jack began.

"If you're standing behind her," I explained, "and you do it right—barely touching her," I said, making my voice low and soft, "your arms lightly encircling her, your hands almost—*almost* touching her breasts, your cheek just grazing her cheek, your quivering mouth close, so close, making her wild for you to— red light, red light. Stop, Jack! Jeez, didn't you see it?"

"You're giving me a lot of different directions, Carly."

"You okay, Harry?" I asked. "Maybe you had better buckle your seat belt."

Harry nodded. His face was pink again.

"Now where was I. . . . Oh, yeah, your cheek just grazing her cheek—"

Jack glanced in the rearview mirror. "You don't have to go on. I think Harry and I've both got the picture."

"Great. We're almost there. Turn right. It's at the end of this dark street. Since you're new around here, you probably want to take note of where the dark streets are. It's lucky Heather lives on one. Not that you need it right away, of course, you don't want to come on too strong."

Jack turned onto the dark road, cut the engine, then the lights.

"What?" I said. "What are you doing?"

He didn't answer me right away. Harry rustled around in the backseat.

"What's going on?"

Jack leaned toward me. I guess it was the sudden darkness, but I was very aware of his closeness—that same good smell, the long line of his cheek and strong jaw, the depth of his voice. When he spoke, there was a very tense edge to it.

"Repeat after me. This is not a setup. We're just four friends having a good time."

"We really will have a good time," I said cheerfully.

"Carly." He held my chin with one finger, one light finger, but I felt as if I couldn't move left or right. He held me still with his closeness. "Repeat after me. This is not a setup."

And that's another thing, I wanted to say. When you touch someone like that in the dark . . . but suddenly I realized Jack might have known what he was doing.

"Okay," I said, pulling away from him. "I get the message."

"Good."

We drove on.

Though we were late, Heather was later, which had become routine for our double dates. I gave the usual tour of the patio and swimming pool. Harry was impressed. Jack, however, was one cool customer and continued to be, even when Heather came out in her short, tight skirt, with her hair falling soft and golden around her face. That was all right. Heather loved his lack of interest. When he pulled the ribbon around my loose ponytail, telling me it was slipping out, she drank it up. I began to believe that Jack knew exactly what he was doing. As he drove to the fairgrounds, I made Heather give directions so she would overcome her shyness.

I've always loved the Fireman's Carnival; I love the fact that it's always just as I've remembered it. The four of us wandered down a row of booths: glass cases with tumbling buttered popcorn, grills with sizzling sausage, and all those sticky tornadoes of pink cotton candy. There were penny pitches and basketball tosses and darts and hoops. There were tables full of second hand junk that no sane person would buy, except perhaps my father. And beyond it all were spokes of light, the grind of machinery, and piercing screams.

"Rides first, then food," Harry suggested. He had finally perked up and taken over his usual scout leader role.

"The roller coaster!" I exclaimed, almost breaking into a run. "Do you like them?"

"When I was a kid," Jack said, keeping up with me, "I asked my mother to put one in the backyard."

"This is a small one, but they send you around three times."

"Maybe this one would have fit," he said. The others hurried behind us.

I had to jockey a bit to get us all in the right places—Harry and me in the first car, which is my favorite spot, Jack and Heather cozy in the second.

Jack told a Hershey Park roller coaster horror story, which I'm pretty sure he made up. I told a Busch

Gardens one, which I definitely made up. We kept one-upping each other while we waited for others to board. Heather laughed politely.

Then all our heads jerked back and we were off. Oh, there's nothing like a roller coaster, the slow climb up, the rush down, then up again, then hurtling down, swish left, swish right.

"No hands," Jack whooped behind me.

I raised my hands high in the air and kept them there, feeling as if I could take off.

"No feet!" Jack hollered.

"What?" I turned around laughing. My hair whipped over my head, the silk ribbon slipping out. Jack snagged it midair.

My loose hair felt as if it had a hurricane in it—I couldn't get a hold of it. I reached back over my shoulder for my ribbon. Jack leaned forward, but our hands couldn't quite touch. I turned to look at him. He was laughing at my wild hair, then smiling at me, his eyes holding my eyes, brilliant with the wind. We just kept looking at each other, tracks rushing beneath us.

Then the cars screeched to a halt. "Ride over," I muttered and stepped unsteadily onto the platform. Harry gave me a hand, and Heather and Jack followed us down the ramp. I saw that my ribbon was looped tightly around Jack's fingers.

"Need a comb?" Heather asked, helpfully removing the ribbon from Jack's hand.

"Got one, thanks."

My small-toothed comb did nothing for the tangled mess. I tied the ribbon on as best as I could, patting my hair down self-consciously.

"We need something calm," said Harry.

"The Ferris wheel," Heather suggested, and we headed that way.

When we got to the front of the line, Jack pushed ahead and got on with Harry. Heather and I stood there looking at each other.

"He's kind of different, isn't he?" Heather said.

"Jack? Yeah."

We climbed into the car together, and the attendant slammed down the bar.

"Does Luke know Jack's interested in you?" Heather asked.

"He isn't," I replied quickly. "Well, at least I don't think he is," I added, realizing too late that it would add to Jack's mystique.

"Are you still interested in Luke?"

"I'm still waiting for that first kiss," I said.

"Oh."

I felt as if Heather was crowding me, though we were sitting on opposite sides of the padded bench, with space for another person in between. We had ridden this wheel every year—when we were little, sitting close at the center, holding hands.

"Well, you know, Carly, I'm really—"

"Happy for me, I know." When she looked hurt, I added, "Friends can read minds." Then I changed the subject to her dance lessons.

There was a guy in Heather's class whom she thought was kind of cute. As we rode in circles, she talked about him. I knew better than to get my hopes up. She said he kept hanging around her. Too bad I couldn't give him a little advice; too bad I couldn't tell him to date me first.

When we got off, Jack wanted to try the basketball throw.

"The hoops are small," I warned him.

"Oh, I'd love a bear!" said Heather.

Jack spent three dollars trying, then I won her the bear. I thought he might be mad—you know how macho guys can get—but he just grinned.

"Here," said Harry, dropping bills into my hand. "Three more bucks. See if you can win one for Joelle and her baby."

I looked up at him, touched by his thoughtfulness. "I'll give it a whirl."

I won on the second dollar, and he picked out the animal, a round-faced panda, her big paws wrapped lovingly around a clinging baby.

After we put the stuffed animals in the car, Harry said he wanted to do the haunted house. The Firemen's House of Fear had to be one of the tackiest places around, plastic bodies bleeding plastic blood, baying hounds whose glowing eyes were red Christmas bulbs, and a very bad sound track. But you walked through the place, which was fun. And sometimes they used live spooks, especially in the dark rooms. The blackened rooms—where there was nothing, but you kept thinking there must be—were probably the only scary part. A few people had trouble finding their way out of them.

When we passed the baying hounds, the graveyard, and the room of ghosts that floated in the wind of small, rattling fans, we were still in line—Jack, Heather, Harry, me. Then we went through a door and plunged into darkness. We stumbled around, reaching out for each other. I grasped a great big hand—Harry's, I hoped—some people have come out bonded to the wrong person. Then Jack's. I was sure it was his hand—I don't know how—I just was.

Then someone who had been hiding in the dark came wailing and hurtling through our line, scattering us. I bumped around but had been in the house enough to have an idea where the door was. As I approached it, I knew Jack was standing there. He was very close. I could smell him.

"Carly," he whispered.

"Sorry, no," I whispered back, trying to disguise my voice.

He laughed softly. "I think the door's this way." Then he took my hand.

Maybe we should have called out to the others, but we didn't. The next chamber was just as dark. Jack and I held onto each other and felt our way around the walls. I felt something soft, but I couldn't remember any curtains there from years past. Then the spook leaped out and I shrieked. Jack grasped my hand hard and pulled me close.

I guess nothing livens up a haunted house more than real, live human screams. The spook pulled my hair and laid icy fingers on the back of my neck. I buried my scream in Jack's chest. His arms wrapped around me. He held me so tightly against him, I could feel the laughter rumbling up in him and his breath on my cheek. I could feel how his knees and his thighs measured against my knees and thighs. I felt the warmth of the whole length of his body.

And for the first time in years I remembered the warm, squirming monster I had patted curiously in a dark room of this haunted house. I realized now what

I couldn't figure out when I was seven: it was a couple making out! I pulled away from Jack and almost fell through the door into the Chamber of Horrors.

The luridly lit chamber was a welcome relief. If I was blushing, well, the red light made us both look that way. I glanced at Jack, then turned quickly to the setups: a soldier being stretched on the rack, a woman standing by a guillotine, holding her own head, and a guy lying on a bed of nails. I stared down at the plastic bed as if fascinated by it. Jack came up behind me, standing very close. I moved a little to the side.

Then I heard Heather's voice. "I told you which way it was, Harry."

Jack and I turned around.

"Hi, guys," Harry greeted us.

"But you wouldn't believe me," Heather continued. "We could have been in there forever."

Harry shrugged and smiled. "I wish we could bring our kids here," he said to Jack and me. "It's just scary enough for them."

"Did you hear somebody really scream?" Heather asked, giggling.

"That was me," I admitted.

She looked at me with surprise. "You? Carly, you were never one of those girls who screamed."

I felt my cheeks get hot.

"Maybe she's never been afraid of anything till now," Jack said, watching me.

Several people entered the chamber then, so we moved on, making it through a cobwebby room and out into the clear carnival night.

On the next two rides, I sat with Harry. It didn't take much jockeying around; Heather had decided that Jack was intriguing. She directed most of her conversation toward him, and he listened the way he always does—smiling easily, laughing lightly. For the drive home, I quickly climbed in the backseat with Harry. When we pulled up in front of Heather's house, I called up to Jack, "Maybe you should walk Heather to the front door."

He glanced at me in the rearview mirror. I could see only his eyes, which were dark and unreadable. "Sure."

The long walk up to Heather's house was lined with bushes, and an old laurel shielded the front door. All you could see was light coming from a lamp above and a lot of leaves. Not that I was looking to see anything else.

"Carly?" Harry asked, touching my arm as if he had been trying to get my attention.

I tore my eyes away from the bushes. "What?"

"I was wondering if you thought—well, I wanted to make sure you thought Joelle would like to have the mother and baby bear."

I could hear the concern in his voice.

"I don't know the whole story," Harry continued, "and I'm not asking to be told it, but from what I could tell, she wasn't jumping for joy about being pregnant."

"You've got that right," I said, my eyes drifting back toward the bushes with the overhead light.

"I think it could be a hard time for her, and I don't want to make it harder."

I forced myself to turn back to Harry. "I think it's awfully nice of you to think of Joelle when we're out having fun. And the fact is, these days, you can't tell what will make her happy. So all a person can do is something really nice like that, and hope it makes things a little better for her."

Harry nodded.

"She's still in love with him," I said, shaking my head. "People get crazy when they fall in love."

"It happens to the best of us," Harry replied with a sigh. "Sometimes when we least expect it."

I glanced at my watch and turned back toward the front door. I could have walked Heather to and from that door four times in the length of time she and Jack were taking. Was she pulling the old lost key trick, or was Jack the one who couldn't bear to say good-bye? After an evening of small glances and few words while they checked each other out, the spark must have ignited during the last two rides.

I tapped my foot against the back of the car seat. I played with the buckle of my seat belt. I closed my eyes and tried to imagine Luke's face, but every time I pictured it, I saw him with his eyes closed, wearing the gown in Disney's *Sleeping Beauty*. I squeezed shut my eyes and tried to imagine him kissing me good night with a long, tender kiss—the way Jack was probably kissing Heather right now.

My eyes were still shut when Jack pulled open the car door. He got in and turned around to look at Harry and me. I could think of nothing to say; apparently, neither could Jack. And Harry was in another world. The three of us rode home in silence. At my house, Harry walked me to the front door, glanced up at the only light in an upstairs window, then put the panda bears in my hand. He walked away, forgetting to say good night.

Maybe I caught it from Harry, I thought, as I unlocked the door. Maybe from Joelle—something was going around, and I didn't like it—this small, indefinable ache of the heart.

TEN

"Eugene," I said at lunchtime the next day, "please remove the fork from April's hair and put it in the trash."

"Why?" he asked me.

"Because it clashes with her barrettes."

"Everybody's a critic," Jack whispered. "I think it looks nice."

"Uh-huh." I tried to move on, but Jack caught me by the arm. He and I'd had little time to talk that day. I had deliberately come in early, fetched the equipment I needed, and slipped out before he had arrived. I'd been avoiding Harry too. I've never been good at lying face-to-face, even when it was the polite thing to do, so I'd left him a note saying how much Joelle liked the bears.

The truth was Joelle had squinted at the bears as if I had brought home a pair of aliens. Then she'd stuck them high on the shelf where her old books on African cultures were gathering dust. She had waited up last night so that she could deliver the phone report.

"You've got three messages," she'd announced as soon as I'd stepped inside the door.

After having listened to two girls who were hot and heavy for Jack, I'd cut off the machine.

Joelle had reached over and clicked it on again. It had been a message from Luke. He was sorry about Monday night. He was hoping I was free Saturday night. Did I like comedy clubs? He did. How about dinner and a comedy club? He left his return number.

"That's what you've been waiting for, isn't it?" Joelle had asked.

"Yeah," I'd said. "Sure." Wasn't it?

"So," Jack said to me now, his hand on my arm, pulling me back to the present, "do you have plans this weekend?"

"Yup. I do. Table four, get the sponge. You've left enough for a kingdom of flies."

"With Luke?" Jack asked.

"Eggbeaters," I said, because I was so used to correcting him.

He laughed. "Whatever. I have an idea," he told me. "What if we make it a double date? You and Luke, me and Heather?"

I stared at him.

"It was just an idea," Jack said.

"Maybe you don't get it," I replied. "The whole point of finding someone perfect for Heather is to keep her from latching onto the guy I'm dating."

"I think it's you who doesn't get it," Jack replied. "Luke and Heather would never make it as a couple. They're both too self-centered to get along for more than a day or two. Think about it, Carly. If both of them are soaking up attention, who's going to give it?"

"You don't even know Luke," I said hotly.

"I know his kind."

"He doesn't soak up attention," I insisted. "He doesn't ask for it. He's just gotten used to it. If you had his body, you would too."

Jack was silent for a moment. "Probably," he said, one side of his mouth drawing up. "Okay, okay. Just give me Heather's number." He handed me a pen and paper bag.

"Eugene," he called, "take the fork out of Janet's hair. It matches her dress very nicely, but she doesn't like it."

I scribbled the number on the bag and handed it back to him.

"Have a great time with Luke," he said, looking into my eyes, holding me still for a moment.

"Thanks. I will," I replied, pulling away. I mean, a real date with Luke Hartly—that was what I had been waiting for, wasn't it?

"*What* are you *waiting* for?" the comedian asked in an exaggerated voice, and Luke howled.

I was waiting for his kiss. I knew that one long, tender, soul-wrapping kiss would change everything. I believed it the way I'd believed last Monday that being alone with Luke would change everything.

Earlier, we had been alone for dinner at a cozy table for two. If only Rita's Health Bar & Buy hadn't smelled so strange. While Luke talked about last week's training, then training for the week coming up—all of which sounded pretty much the same to me—I stared at row after row of brown bottles with vitamins. I poked at sprouts, which lay under a blanket of organic lettuce and appeared to be multiplying there. I longed for a Quarter Pounder with Cheese.

"I figured you'd like this place," Luke said. "You're kind of an athlete."

"I *am* an athlete," I told him.

I guess he didn't hear me, because an hour and a half later, he was laughing wildly at the comedian's jokes about women jocks. He didn't laugh quite so much at the next performer, a woman in boots and a leopard skirt who had a few interesting things to say about men. For my part, I went wild stuffing my face with trays full of tacos and cheese, suddenly ravenous for anything with high salt and fat content. Then he took me home.

"I had a really nice time," Luke said as he walked me to the door. I was tempted to look at my watch, to see if I could make good night last as long as Heather and Jack did.

"I really like talking to you, Carly," Luke went on, his eyes shining soft green in the lamplight.

I smiled and waited.

"You listen. And you're so pretty," he added shyly.

I felt myself melting. "Thanks, Luke."

Then he pulled me close. "Carly," he whispered.

This is it, this is it, I thought, *the kiss!*

And then I thought, *he smells wrong.* Maybe it was Rita's Health Bar mixed with his aftershave, I don't know, but it was all wrong. His lips suddenly touched mine. His strong hands held my arms—like the handles on a pommel horse. I expected him to vault at any moment. But he held on and pressed his mouth to mine, in a long, long kiss. It was like kissing a plastic doll—Heather and I had done a lot of that when we were twelve.

"Well, thanks," I said, backing away.

"Want to do something next Saturday?" he asked, a little breathless. "We can go to Rita's again. Come by the gym to watch me this week. You want to?"

I nodded halfheartedly. "I'll call you."

"At this point, it doesn't look good, Steve," I said on Sunday night. "Yeah. Really. Sorry. Bye."

I clicked off the cordless phone and sat back in the porch chair. "Open your eyes, Steve-O," I mumbled. "Look next door." But even I had had no idea that the perfect match would be so perfect.

I had called Heather at one o'clock Saturday, wondering if Jack had asked her out yet, certain that she would shy away from his bold invitation.

But she was already with him.

I expected a return message from her when I got home Saturday night.

There wasn't one.

Probably because they had stayed out past midnight—her mother gave me that piece of information when I called noontime Sunday. Heather would have told me herself, but she was out with Jack again. Her mother said she'd have Heather call me as soon as she got home.

Now I sat with the phone in my lap, watching the fireflies wander in the dark grass. This was an all-time record for Heather. She had never spent so much time with one guy, especially one who wasn't dating me. What were she and Jack doing? I gazed out into the summer night, feeling that small, indefinable ache again. Maybe they were watching fireflies, wishing on one like a star.

102

I hardly knew what I wished for anymore.

Except that I wished Joelle had gone with my parents to their weeklong conference. They had left me with a list of emergency phone numbers—doctors, neighbors, relatives, their hotel, the conference center—as if I were her baby-sitter or something. It's true that during their last literary conference, my big sister had managed to set the kitchen curtains on fire and kept calling 119. But she was supposed to be growing into a mother, and I was getting tired of being the responsible one.

I had mentioned this last night, and she hadn't spoken to me since. Maybe we wouldn't speak all week. I felt at odds with the entire world.

A chair scraped back.

"You keep sighing," Joelle said.

I turned my head slightly. "I'm just breathing loudly. If it bothers you, sit somewhere else."

"How'd it go last night?" she asked, pulling her chair closer.

"Fine."

"Just fine?"

"Isn't fine good enough?" I snapped.

"You know, I made a pan of brownies for the church's bake sale." It was normal for Joelle to skip from topic to topic.

"Good. Did they sell them all?"

"You ate them all, Carly, last night when you came in."

"Oh. Jeez. I'm sorry . . . I'll make a donation."

"A chocolate orgy and sighs," she said. "I'd say you've got it bad."

"You don't know what you're talking about."

Joelle sat back in her chair, stretching her bare feet

out in front of her. She was hardly showing, but she had already adopted that hands-resting-on-tummy routine.

"I ate a giant bag of Reese's Pieces after my first date with Sam," she told me.

"Well, don't draw any conclusions, Joelle. I am not falling in love with Luke."

"Luke? Oh, I didn't think you were falling for *him*," she replied. "I was sure my little sister had better taste than that!"

I glanced sideways. Joelle had this all-knowing look on her face, and I was afraid she really did know the truth that I could barely admit to myself.

She smiled at me. "What I didn't know was how soon you'd figure out which guy you really wanted."

I sighed. "Obviously, not soon enough."

ELEVEN

"**R**UNNER'S COMING HOME, coming home, coming home! There's a throw to the plate. Come on, Miguel!" I shouted.

Miguel reared back and gave it all he had. All the other players in our noontime game were imaginary.

"Out! Whooeee—watch out Ken Griffey, Jr.," I said. "We've got an all-star outfielder right here."

Miguel's face shone. Every buck I had spent on a small left-hander's glove was worth it. After discussing the situation with Harry and Anna, I had bought the glove, then pulled Miguel from Monday's lunch period to field some balls. I hoped to boost his confidence by helping him do what he did best; that would make everything else a little easier for him.

We had been playing hard for thirty-five minutes. I glanced up at the sky and beckoned him in. The wind was picking up and there was just a scrape of blue left in the northeast.

"Please," Miguel begged, "one more fly ball."

I walloped the ball and watched him race across the field. He was fast as a cat and every bit as graceful. I'd never seen a little kid with so much ability.

"Please, Miss Carly, one more," he called to me again.

I shook my head. "I promised the big boss you'd eat lunch."

He stood out in the field for a moment, his short brown legs planted firmly, pounding his fist in his glove—the first bit of resistance I had seen in Miguel.

"Come on, kiddo. It's going to rain."

He trudged in slowly. I opened up our bag of peanut butter sandwiches, and napkins flew up in our faces. Miguel sat close to me on the bleachers, gobbling up the squishy bread till the crust wrapped like a smile around his face. He put it down and reached for another half sandwich.

"You know, Miguel, eating might be easier if you took off your glove."

He looked up at me, his dark eyes searching mine to see if I really meant it, then he smiled and kept the glove on.

"How come you don't get mad at me when I mess up?" he asked, his mouth full.

"Get mad? Why should I?" I replied. "I mess up all the time. Everybody does. Nobody wants to, but everybody does."

"José doesn't," Miguel said firmly.

"Who's José?"

"A boyfriend," he said.

"Your mother's?"

He nodded.

"Do you like José?" I asked.

Miguel turned away from me. "Mm-hmm."

I didn't believe him. "Does he live with you?"

"Sometimes. Where do you live?" Miguel asked. "Do you have a backyard?"

"About three miles from here. Yes, I have a backyard."

"Do you live near Mr. Jack?" he wondered.

"Mr. Jack lives near the golf course, the place where we all go swimming."

He licked the peanut butter off his fingers. "I wish I could live with Mr. Jack."

"You want to take up golf?" I joked.

"He's nice," Miguel said simply.

I nodded and hoped we wouldn't have to talk too much about Jack. I had thought about him enough yesterday and had carefully avoided him all morning. Then Miguel had provided me a welcome escape from lunch with him and Anna.

"He says things that make me feel good inside."

"Does he," I said softly.

"Sometimes he plays his guitar for us. And he tells us stories, lots of them about magic. I think he believes in it. I almost believe. Do you?"

"I used to," I said, slipping my sandwich back in its plastic bag.

"Aren't you hungry?" he asked.

"Guess not. I ate a lot of brownies over the weekend," I told him.

"Yeah? Any in here?" He reached into the paper bag.

"Just cookies."

"That's okay." He smiled, then lifted his arm suddenly, pointing with the bag still in his hand. "Hey, there's Mr. Jack."

I looked quickly over my shoulder.

"Who's that?" Miguel asked. "Who's that girl with him?"

"A friend of Mr. Jack's. Her name is Heather."

Why didn't I say she was my friend too?

Miguel and I watched the two of them as they walked along a path that skirted the field. I doubted that they had seen us—they were probably too engrossed in each other.

"Is she a girlfriend?"

"Looks like it," I said.

"Hey, Mr.—"

"Shhh! Don't call him. He's talking with his friend."

What if he kissed his friend? I thought. It would serve Jack right if his second-graders stopped painting pictures of the crazy counselor with the red hair and started painting him making out with a blonde.

Heather and Jack disappeared behind a tree—*cripe, they spent enough time behind bushes and trees,* I thought—but really the path just wound that way, in the direction of the building where Heather took dance lessons. A few moments later Jack emerged, apparently having parted with Heather, walking alone in our direction.

"Hey, Mr. Jack! Hey, look! Look what Miss Carly found for me to use."

Miguel ran toward Jack. I stayed where I was. Jack's face broke into a huge grin. He leaned down to talk to Miguel and examine the glove. It didn't fit on Jack's hand, but he waved it around from his fingertips and pretended to be fielding a ball. Miguel imitated him. Then Jack called for a ball as if he were trying to catch a high pop-up. He windmilled his arms. "I got it! I got it! I got it! I don't," he said. Miguel dropped on the grass, laughing.

Jack pulled him up, then put his hand on the little boy's shoulder, resting it there. I felt a momentary twinge—I wished I was somebody who could laugh with Jack, someone he wanted to reach out to and touch gently. It was like watching him with Anna, that silly momentary twinge of jealousy when I saw their ease and closeness with each other.

"Get a grip, Carly," I muttered to myself.

Jack put the glove on Miguel's head, then looked down the first-base line at me, smiling. I gave him a quick smile back, then stood up and gathered together the blowing lunch stuff.

"Hey, Carly."

"Hey, Jack."

"It looks like you guys have been having a good time."

"Sure have," I said, avoiding his eyes. "Miguel's a star. I hope he remembers us when he gets to the majors."

Miguel beamed.

"How's Heather?" I asked.

"Heather?"

"Your girlfriend," said Miguel.

Jack blinked. "Oh. Okay. We missed you at lunch."

Sure, I thought and glanced up at the sky. The rain couldn't come soon enough.

"I guess you know I went out with her over the weekend," Jack continued.

And out, and out, and out, I thought. "Yeah, her mother told me," I replied. We began walking three abreast to the student center. "That's terrific. Really terrific."

"How was your weekend?" Jack asked.

"Oh, it was terrific too."

"She ate a lot of brownies," said Miguel.

Jack laughed. "Eggbeaters likes brownies?"

"No, I do," I replied crisply.

Jack leaned forward a little, as if he were trying to read my face. He tried to get me to look back, tried to get me to meet his eyes.

"If we don't hurry," I said, "we'll all get drenched." *Please rain,* I prayed, *please rain now.*

Someone must have been listening. A flash of lightning followed, and the skies opened. I grabbed Miguel's hand. He squealed like a little pig, and we dashed for the student center. Miguel and I didn't stop running till we were among the other kids who were emerging from the cafeteria. Eugene pulled on my wet hair. Janet demanded to know where I had been. April offered me two of her barrettes. I was glad to be among the kids, who were laughing and talking a mile a minute. I was glad to have them swarm around me and keep me safe from the questioning eyes of Jack.

That evening it was still raining, pinging against the aluminum siding of the family room, rattling a loose gutter. Joelle and I sat side by side on the couch, watching one of the dumbest sitcoms I had ever seen. *This is how we'll end up,* I thought, *Joelle and me, two unmarried sisters living together, watching stupid sitcoms, raising Buddy.*

"Should I make brownies?" Joelle asked.

"No." I guessed I'd been sighing again.

"So what did Luke say when you told him you were busy next Saturday?" Joelle wanted to know.

He had called right after dinner, and she had listened till I switched to the cordless and stood inside the coat closet. But I did it just to annoy her. I really didn't care what she knew about Luke.

"He asked about Sunday."

"And you said?" she prompted.

"That I was busy."

"And he said?"

I picked up the remote and began clicking through the channels. "How about Monday, but he had to be in bed by ten o'clock."

My sister put her hand over mine. "You know, Luke may not be smart enough to take a hint."

"Tell me about it," I said, surfing even faster. "I finally told him straight out that I didn't want to date him."

"Was he crushed?"

"He asked if I wanted to come watch him at his next meet."

She hooted, and I had to laugh a little.

"Oh, Carl," she said.

"Oh, Joe." We hadn't used those names for a long time.

"So, did you tell Jack that you and Sleeping Beauty are no longer an item?"

"Why would I tell Jack?" I asked, prickling. We were back at the stupid sitcom. I glared at the actors. "I thought you were keeping track of everything that's going on, Joelle. You should know he's dating Heather."

"I know. But something like that's never stopped *her* before, has it?"

I stood up. Maybe I did need chocolate. "No—because the guy's always been interested in her. But

111

Jack's not interested in me." My voice wavered. "So, lucky Heather."

Joelle got up to follow me, then sank back against the sofa.

"Are you all right?"

"Yeah, sure," she said, waving her hand.

Her color hadn't looked good since the time I'd arrived home. "You don't look all right. What's wrong?"

She shrugged. "Who knows? My body doesn't act or feel like my own body anymore. It's like it's been possessed."

I frowned and wrapped my arms around myself. I felt as if my heart was possessed. *First, someone steals your heart,* I thought, *then everything else starts slipping away.*

"Want anything from the kitchen?"

"Whatever you're having is okay with me," she said.

I came back with stale Hostess Twinkies and milk. Her face was about the color of the two-percent.

"Let's watch a video," she suggested.

I opened the door of the glass cabinet. "What do you want to see?" I know—my agreeableness was amazing. I was worried about her.

"*The Way We Were.*"

"What?" The film was part of my parents' collection and a horrible tearjerker. "Why?"

"So we can cry and feel sorry for somebody else," Joelle suggested.

"But I hate that movie. I hate Barbra Streisand's character. She's got wild hair, is incredibly pigheaded, and falls ridiculously in love with a hunk she was never meant for."

My sister shrugged. "Yeah, well." I was surprised that she could resist a remark like, "Look in the mirror, Carl." She must have been feeling really rotten.

I put the cassette into the VCR and got out the tissues.

We were halfway through when Joelle leaned over and hit the stop button on the remote. "Think I need a bathroom break."

She got to her feet a little unsteadily.

"Joelle?"

"I'm fine."

I stared at the back of her loose dress and went cold all over. There was a large red stain on it.

Joelle pulled the shift around to look at it. "Oh," she said, and sat back down. "What do we do now?" She looked as if she were going to faint.

"Call 119?"

She frowned.

"That was a joke," I muttered, and ran for the phone.

TWELVE

"I'M NOT TIRED," I insisted to Harry at lunchtime the next day. "I slept some at the hospital," I added. "Don't make me go home. Joelle and I were together for nineteen hours. That's about as much as either of us can take."

The doctor had released Joelle at nine A.M., sentencing her to complete bed rest. By ten we had started getting on each other's nerves. At eleven, Joelle had said, "I wish you'd go to work." We'd argued about it, then I'd telephoned our twelve-year-old neighbor. Mandy was glad to come over and watch the soaps for a couple bucks.

"Did you call your parents?" Harry asked me now, rocking back in his office chair.

"Joelle wouldn't let me. I didn't know what to do, Harry. She got so upset, started crying, and begged me not to. I was afraid I'd make it worse. I mean, I know it's my fault. I've made her feel like she's a lot of trouble. It's all my fault."

"It's nobody's fault, Carly. And you can't expect Joelle to be thinking clearly right now. You've got to keep your own head on straight. What did the doctor say?"

"To keep her in bed. If she starts to bleed again, call him immediately. He'll check on her tomorrow."

"Can you handle that?"

I nodded.

"Good," Harry said, then scribbled on a piece of paper. "Here's my home number. Call me anytime, for any reason, even if you just want another person around. Call me at three A.M., and I'll be on the way a minute later. I'll bring pizza."

I smiled a little, looked down at the number, then stuffed it in my pocket. "Thanks, Harry."

"And don't worry about the camp sleep-over Thursday night. I'll get a sub," he said. "Where should I send Hau and the kids this afternoon?" It was still raining outside and the fields were soaked. "The old gym?"

I nodded, glad that I'd have Hau's help for one session.

When Hau arrived at the gym, he was carrying a stack of cards his kids had made. I opened each one. "Hope You Get Good," I read. "Thanks, Tam. Thanks, everyone. My sister will love these." Even if Joelle stuck them on the highest shelf with Harry's bears, the homemade cards sure cheered *me* up.

Later, when Harry brought over the second-graders, they marched in like little angels.

"Just goes to show," Harry whispered, "they can behave when they want to."

None of them picked on Miguel that day. Whether it was the other kids' good behavior or yesterday's workout that gave him new confidence, I

115

wasn't sure, but Miguel seemed happier and made two baskets, which is a lot for anyone who is three-and-a-half-feet tall. Working with the campers really helped me that afternoon. I was sorry when Harry returned to take them to the bus.

But Harry was making it easy for me, playing usher like that, easier than he knew. I didn't have to face Jack. Jack had seen the angry side of me; he'd believe I was capable of saying mean things to Joelle and getting her upset. He'd give me that probing look; maybe he'd see how frightened I was for her and Buddy. And I couldn't deal with that; I couldn't deal with anyone who made me feel more vulnerable than I already was.

I sat down on the bottom row of bleachers, untying old knots in the string of the ball bag. I like silent gyms. I can pray in old, gray-green gyms with Coke-bottle windows easier than I can in church. I bent over the ball bag, working the knots the way my grandmother used to work the beads of her rosary, praying for Joelle. For me too.

"Carly? Are you okay?"

Heather's voice startled me.

"Sure. Sure. Just putting stuff away."

She toed a yellow line uncertainly, then walked across the court toward me. "How's Joelle?"

"Okay. The doctor's going to check on her again tomorrow. She's a little shook up, but I think she'll be all right."

"How about you?" Heather asked, sitting down beside me.

"Pretty much like Joelle, I guess."

"I'm sorry. It must have been hard for you. I

remember when Mom was in the car accident. Sometimes it's scarier being the person trying to help, than the one who needs it."

I swallowed hard.

"I kept trying to call last night. I was really worried," she said. Her soft gray eyes showed it.

"I know. I got your messages this morning."

"I called Jack. He was worried too."

I rose to round up the basketballs. Heather went to the opposite corner to fetch a stray ball, then mimicked a layup, doing one of her ballet leaps, getting incredible height for her small stature.

"I tell you, the team lost out the day you decided to sign up for dance," I said.

She smiled at me. "I love it. I love what I'm learning here. I owe you, Carly, for not letting me be a quitter."

I grinned back at her. "You're too good to be a quitter."

"I was talking about it last night," she said, "about how you pulled me out of that dancewear store and gave me a speech. I was telling Jack."

I wished she'd stop mentioning him. In Heather's first phone message, before she started getting worried about me, she had wanted to talk about Jack.

"I need some more advice," she said.

I stuffed two balls into the net bag, then held out my hand for the one she was toying with.

"It's about Jack," Heather added.

"What about him?"

"I really like him, Carly." She twisted her long blond hair around her fingers. "I mean *really*."

I nodded.

"He just keeps wanting to see me, and see me again. It's so strange. . . ." she said, shaking her head.

Actually, it was a perfectly normal male response to Heather. The strange part was that Heather kept wanting to see him. I had thought Jack was cocky when he said he didn't need my help in dating, but I realized now that he was used to getting the girl he wanted.

"I'm not sure what to do," Heather said, sighing.

I had this sudden urge to lift the bag of balls over my head, whip it around and around by its string, then let it fly.

"How about enjoy it?" I suggested quietly.

"I wish I could," she told me. "If only I wasn't taking this class with Dan."

"Dan? Who's Dan?"

"Another student. He goes to Kirbysmith and is a wonderful dancer—the teacher says we're perfect together. Since sophomore year of high school he's been steady with the same girl and thought they'd always be a couple. But now that he's met me, he's not so sure."

Of course. A guy with a girlfriend. A college guy committed to the same girl since tenth grade. I wanted to shriek and run up the wooden bleachers.

"Do you think it's okay to date both Dan and Jack at the same time? I would tell them, of course. I wouldn't lead them on and make them think they're each the only one."

"That's good of you," I said.

She heard the tone of my voice and looked at me funny. "I see. You don't think I should."

What could I say? That I thought she was a jerk to keep chasing other people's boyfriends? Hands off Dan? Saying that, I'd steer her back toward Jack.

Which was the right thing to do, of course, because that way she wouldn't be breaking another girl's heart, at least none that she or Jack knew about.

I tried to say it, to tell her not to let Jack slip away, but I just couldn't. "I can't help you this time," I told her at last. "You'll have to decide for yourself."

She looked at me as if I had abandoned her. "Well, I guess you've got a lot on your mind right now," she said, trying to be understanding.

"That's for sure." I stuck my arm through the bleachers, swatting a ball so that it would roll to the end. "Maybe we could talk later."

"Okay," she replied agreeably, turning to leave. "I need to get home and get ready for tonight."

Get ready for who? I wondered a few minutes later, as I retrieved the ball from under the stands. I picked it up and slammed it against the wall, took the rebound and slammed it again.

I raced with it down court, dribbling, switching hands, banging it off the bleachers and catching it again, rushing toward the basket. Layup. *Swish.* I backed up. *Swish.* Backed up. *Swish.* I couldn't miss. Twenty-five-foot jumper—*swish!* I snatched the ball from the backboard, spun toward the far court, and slammed into a six-foot rock—I mean, six-foot-one.

"Charging," Jack said, taking the ball away from me. "I get one shot."

I took the ball back. "I didn't say you could play."

"Court hog," he replied, then shrugged. "I really came to talk."

Just what I didn't want to do. I dribbled away from him and shot the ball. *Swish.* I was hot today. At least, when it came to basketball, I was hot.

"How's your sister?" he asked.

I went for a three-pointer. "Okay." Rebound. "She's home." I hooked it over my head. *Swish.*

"Harry said your parents weren't around this week. You had to drive her to the hospital yourself."

"It was great having a reason to speed," I replied lightly and tossed the ball toward the rim. *Bobble, bobble, swish.* "I was kind of disappointed when I wasn't caught."

"Really," he said.

The truth was I was so shaken I kept shifting into the wrong gear.

"You seem pretty cool about it all."

"Well, it was no big deal." *Swish.* "Just part of having a baby. Joelle was cool too," I lied.

"Well, if there's anything I can do for you," he offered, "anything that might make it easier. . . ."

Go away, I thought. *That will make it easier.* I missed the basket.

The rebound bounced off directly to Jack, and he wouldn't give up the ball.

"I can get another one from the bag," I told him.

"You could, but you're too proud to give up on this one," he said, dribbling away from me.

I scowled at him.

"Twenty-one points," he challenged me. "And since I'm a polite guy, I'll let you have the ball first."

"I don't need the advantage."

"Good," he replied. "Then I'll take it." He drove past me and flipped the ball up nice and easy. "Two–nothing."

"Lucky."

Jack tossed the ball to me. I drove hard, but he was

fast, and I had to pull back out again. I gave him a little fake, just a slight movement with my shoulders. He fell for it. I spun around him and shot. "Two up."

He brought the ball in, and I waited, figuring he could never make it from that distance. *Swish.* "Four–two."

"So," I said, "your mother couldn't get you a roller coaster for the backyard and got you a basketball hoop instead. All your life you've been practicing and waiting for this moment?"

He grinned and walked the ball out to me. He stood very close. Too close. "All my life I've been waiting for this moment."

I faked around him. A half step later he caught up with me.

The longer we played, the harder we played, and the closer, tracking each other, hands resting on each other's backs, reaching over and under and around, sweaty arm against sweaty arm. I was aware of every brush. He was making me crazy—he seemed to be every which way I turned. I was winning 12 to 8, but I felt as if I was losing.

We went up for a rebound and came down in a heap—came down like an octopus, two bodies slammed into one with eight arms and legs.

I lay on top of him, stunned.

"You okay?" he asked.

I tried to climb off of him, but he held me for a moment. It didn't mean anything. It was the way you'd hold a child you had accidentally knocked down.

"I'm fine," I said. "How about you?"

"Great."

121

I pulled free and crawled a few feet away. "I, uh, don't want to play anymore."

"I hurt you," he said, sitting up quickly.

"No. It's just been a long day. A forty-eight-hour day. Yesterday never quite ended."

He studied my face. We were both a little out of breath.

"Are you sure there isn't anything I can do? I could come over and stay with Joelle for a while if you wanted to go out. You know, if you and Eggbeaters had a hot date," he added.

"Thanks, but no thanks. My parents will be back Saturday."

He continued to study me with those intense blue eyes. His dark hair curled damp around his face. I watched as he picked up his T-shirt to wipe off the sweat. I was really losing it, wanting to touch his damp hair, and peeking at his chest.

"So how's it going with Heather?" I asked.

"Well, it *was* going okay, but I think she's starting to lose interest." He smiled a little. "You knew that would happen. Go ahead and say it, Carly, you told me so."

"Listen," I said, "you've done a zillion times better than anyone else. I mean, Heather's never spent two days and two nights with the same guy and come back for lunch. Don't give up now."

He looked up at me, and for a moment his eyes seemed a different color. They looked so unhappy, so disappointed.

A good friend would help bring together two people she cared about, I thought—even if she'd discovered she cared about her new friend a whole lot more than her old friend. "Don't get down about it, Jack. I know something that could help you out."

Then I told him about Heather wanting to date the guy in her class as well as Jack. "I know it probably hurts your feelings, but if you stay cool and beat her to the punch, if you announce first that you think you should date other people, well then—hah!" I said with grim satisfaction.

"Hah," he repeated softly.

"You've got her! Oh, she'll go out with that other guy, but all she'll be able to think about and wonder about is you."

It was like the sun coming up in his eyes. "It's a good idea," he said at last. "How about this Saturday night?"

"Well, if I were you, I'd tell Heather right away, but I guess you could wait till the weekend to take out somebody else."

"That's what I'm saying," he said. "Are you free?"

"What?"

"Can you do it Saturday night? Don't worry. I'll explain to Eggbeaters. He'll probably think it's funny."

But it wasn't funny. The thought of spending an entire evening with Jack, helping him win Heather, made me miserable. I got up from the floor, picked up the basketball, and started walking toward the ball bag. "I don't know. I don't think it's such a good idea."

"Carly," he said, following close behind, "you know that as soon as Heather finds out I'm with you, she'll be incredibly jealous and interested."

I dropped the ball in the bag.

"I helped you out when you were shooting for

Eggbeaters," he reminded me. "It'd be just for a night, or maybe two or three, whatever it takes. I'll take you to some fun places." He put his hand on my arm. "Can't you pretend we've got something going?"

I knew I owed him. I trudged across the gym floor, dragging the bag behind me. "Sure. We can always pretend."

THIRTEEN

JUST AS I expected, Joelle asked me to put the kids' cards up on the shelf with Harry's panda bears. However, she looked at each one first and smiled once or twice.

"'Get Ready!'" she read and held the drawing up for me to see.

"He means 'Get Well,'" I told her.

"I don't know," Joelle replied, resting her hand on her stomach. "Get ready might be the right wish for me."

After dinner, when she was absorbed in *Wheel of Fortune,* I moved the bears down to a lower shelf and surrounded them by the cards, displaying them as decoratively as I could. I also picked out three books on anthropology and West African cultures and slipped them between the magazines in the pile next to her bed.

In the morning I left her fixed up like a princess— breakfast on a bedside table, a freezer chest packed with snacks and juice, books and magazines and the

TV remote, letter paper and colored pens, a Walkman, batteries, portable phone, and list of phone numbers—all within reach. Our neighbor, Mandy, was supposed to come over at eleven-thirty.

I was late for work on a day that we were going on a field trip. When I finally climbed onto the singing, vibrating bus, the kids gave me a big cheer.

"They really like you!" Pamela said. She was sitting in the front seat next to Jack.

I nodded and smiled a little.

"Hey, Carly." Jack grinned at me. I guess he was as happy as the kids to see the girl who could make his dreams come true—with someone else.

"Hey, Jack." I moved on to the back to sit with Anna. Hau was going to follow the school bus in his own car, so he could give the counselors a ride back to campus when we sent the kids home at the end of the day.

A trip to the Baltimore Museum of Art was Harry's idea. He thought that the schools would take our campers to places like the National Aquarium and the zoo, where the exhibits would be fascinating and the kids naturally well behaved. So we should dare to offer some culture. Of course, Harry was staying behind at Kirbysmith, collecting bedrolls being dropped off by scout troops for tomorrow's sleep-over. It was the rest of us who had to inform museum guards of stopped-up toilets, apologize for alarms going off, and explain about art and polite behavior when the kids pointed and hooted at nudes.

But the day went better than expected. After a tour with two museum guides who said they enjoyed a challenge, the campers played Treasure Hunt. Jack and Anna had made up lists of people and objects to be found in museum pictures, and the kids eagerly searched from room to room. Then we had lunch in the pretty park across from the main entrance. Afterward, we let the kids run and scream their lungs out for an hour. When they were calmer, we took them back into the museum, along with a supply of paper and pencils, to draw what inspired them.

When we finally got the campers back on the bus with our trustworthy driver, the five of us set off for Kirbysmith in Hau's car. I rode up front and after one block could not keep my eyes open. My head bobbed and banged against the window. *Must be catching,* I thought. *Sleeping Beauty disease.* Pamela asked me something, then I heard Jack say quietly, "Shhh. She's asleep."

But I woke up quickly a half hour later when we were back on campus and I saw the note left for me on the camp office door.

> Carly,
>   Joelle called. Have gone to your house.
>   Don't worry—I've called the doctor.
>   I'll stay with her until you get back.
>   Harry

"I'll drive you home," Jack said, reading over my shoulder.

"Thanks, but I've got the car this week."

"Even so, it might help to have someone with you."

I glanced back at him.

"I mean, if you drive anything like the way you bike," he added, trying to turn his offer into a joke.

"I can handle this."

But maybe I couldn't, I thought, when I got home and saw my sister asleep in her bed of pillows, looking pale and years younger than nineteen. Harry was sprawled out on my bed, reading one of Joelle's West Africa books. He smiled at me, glanced over at her, then walked me silently downstairs.

"The doctor said she's all right and can be up in a couple of days, if she takes it easy," he told me.

"Why'd she call you? Where was the baby-sitter?" I asked.

"No one else was here when I arrived," Harry said, sitting me down on the sofa. "She called the office about twelve-thirty and said she had fallen. She was scared."

"How did she fall? Did she black out?"

"She said she slipped on a scatter rug."

"A scatter rug?" I thought for a moment, then leaped up from the sofa and hurried into the hall. "We have wall-to-wall upstairs," I told Harry, who had followed me. I pointed to the small rug on the bare wood floor. "She *knew* she was not supposed to do steps!" I said angrily. "She *knew* she was supposed to stay upstairs!"

"Why don't I hang around for a while?" Harry suggested. "I'm really enjoying this book."

I leaned against the door frame. "Don't worry. I'll calm down before she wakes up. I just don't know what to do with her, Harry. I'm tired of acting like the older sister around here."

"Maybe she's tired of acting like the younger one," he suggested, "but doesn't know how to stop playing the role. Maybe that's why she's doing things her way, even if it's not the smartest way."

128

Maybe, but I was still feeling angry and worn out from worrying about her. Harry stayed for another hour, and we talked about the kids at camp. I let him take home Joelle's book. Before he left, he gave me his phone number again.

When Joelle woke up, I had dinner ready. She told me the same thing Harry had, then we ate together off bed trays, silently watching TV reruns.

I was being pretty cool. I knew I shouldn't upset her. I kept reminding myself of the time I'd played a basketball game on a hurting ankle without telling the coach I'd sat in the ER most of the night before and had been diagnosed with a hairline fracture. Stubbornness to the point of stupidity ran in our family.

Then the phone rang. It was the girl from next door, the baby-sitter, calling to thank Joelle for letting her go to the mall today and wondering if we wanted her to come over tomorrow.

"I'll call you back," I said.

"Who was that?" Joelle asked innocently.

"Mandy."

"Oh."

"She said thanks for letting her off today. She was wondering if we'd like her to come over tomorrow."

"Whatever you think is best," Joelle said mildly.

"Whatever *I* think is best?" I repeated. "I thought it was best for her to be here *today*. Obviously, you didn't!"

"When she came, she said that her mother made her do it. I didn't think that was fair," Joelle replied. "She was supposed to meet her friends at the mall."

"I don't care if she was supposed to meet the president of the United States."

"I don't want people waiting on me, Carly," Joelle

insisted. "The doctor said I was doing fine." She fussed with the pillows behind her. "I don't need help—I'll be back to normal soon."

"Back to normal? Back to normal?" I could hardly keep from shouting. "I don't think you get it, Joelle. We'll never be back to normal. This is a baby, this is Buddy, not one of those lost cats you brought home, not the bird with the broken wing."

She bit her lip.

"It's not as simple as feeding it and waiting for it to fly away," I went on. "You're going to need help. Big time. So get used to it."

She pressed her lips together stubbornly. It was like looking into a mirror.

"I can't imagine what was so incredibly important that you had to go downstairs," I muttered.

"The photo album. I wanted to look through it. I—I was trying to imagine Buddy. I wanted to see pictures of us as babies."

The albums were in the hall closet. The oldest one was high up on a stack of books.

"You mean," I said slowly, "you were standing on a chair—that nice wobbly one—on that nice slippery rug?"

She didn't reply.

"Joelle!" I exploded. "You're going to make a terrible mother! You can't take care of yourself. How are you going to take care of a kid?"

"What do you care, Carly?" she shot back. "You've never wanted my baby around. Admit it— you were horrified when I first told you about it. Buddy's messed up your plans. And you're mad about it. Now leave us alone."

I swallowed hard. Both of our eyes were burning red.

"I'm calling Mom."

"No, Carly, wait. Don't. Please don't." She tried to pull the paper with the phone numbers out of my hand. "It's just a couple more days."

But I started dialing. I was mixed up about a lot of things, but I knew for dead certain I was in over my head with Joelle.

My parents made reservations for an early morning flight and arrived home noontime Thursday. I was never so glad to see them. I threw my bedroll and backpack in the car and took off for Kirbysmith. The camp sleep-over could not have happened at a better time. I wished I could camp out somewhere all weekend—and cancel the "date" with Jack too.

When I arrived, Harry reviewed the basic strategy of the day. The first-graders were leaving as usual at 3:15. After that, my job was to lead the second- and third-grade kids in games and activities that would thoroughly exhaust them.

I loved it. We ran every possible kind of race. We had jumping and hopping competitions. We chased soccer balls and softballs and Frisbees. After our evening cookout, we had simultaneous games going of Capture the Flag, Steal the Bacon, and Hoopla.

I was running from one game to the other when Jack caught me by the arm.

"The kids are supposed to conk out early, not you," he said.

"Well, we'll see which of us falls asleep first tonight," I replied.

"Want to bet on it?" he asked.

I hesitated.

"Whoever dozes off first, buys dinner Saturday night." He grinned, then held up his pinky.

I know—it's a silly little gesture, but linking fingers had the same effect on me as his turning my face toward him in the dark car. I felt as if somebody had cast a spell, as if time had stalled for a moment. I pulled away and raced off to my next game.

When the games were finally over, it was time for Anna and Jack to work their magic. We sat in a circle on the Commons, close to the wooded area by the stream. We couldn't have a campfire, but the night was alight with fireflies, and the moon came up almost round, a golden egg. To kids who had lived in the neon city all their lives, just being on a grassy field near tall trees and seeing the blue glitter of stars was something. Anna told the kids stories, then Jack got out his guitar.

The kids sang with him, some funny songs he had taught them. Harry clapped his hands and stamped his feet, keeping time. I kept thinking about the stuffed bears and the way Harry stayed with Joelle, when I knew he had a zillion things to do at camp. If only Joelle had fallen for a nice guy like him. But the heart is a traitor. It could make a girl betray her best friend and a guy betray his wife; it could make you betray even the one you loved.

Jack sang a ballad that the kids didn't know, an Irish love song about two people on either side of the sea. I pulled up my knees and rested my arms on them, keeping my face down. I felt a small hand on my back—April, my barrette girl.

Jack sang a happier song, then some gentle lulla-bies. They were comforting; still, their sweetness made me ache inside. The kids near him moved even closer.

Then it was time to organize the kids into bath-room lines and zip them into their bags. We laid the forty sleeping bags close to where we had made our circle, on an open field with a fence along one side. Harry wanted us to work in teams, a pair of us sta-tioned on each of the other three sides. That way, if one of us had to walk a kid to the bathroom, the other counselor would still be there. He took his sister Pamela as his partner, perhaps because she wasn't all that reliable.

"Okay," I said, "Hau and I will be on the opposite side from you."

"Sorry, Hau's with me," Anna said quickly.

I looked at her surprised. "But Hau and I work well as a team."

"It's good to switch around," she replied, smiling but firm.

"Don't look so worried," Jack said. "I'll try to keep it down to a low snore. Besides, you'll be nod-ding off long before I do," he added, reminding me of the bet.

"Terrific," Harry said, clapping his hands to-gether. "Well, folks, good luck, and may we all get thirty minutes of uninterrupted sleep."

Jack and I walked around to our side of the square and laid down our bags about twelve feet away from the kids. They were still talking and giggling, but their voices had begun to lower. Eugene, of course, contin-ued to talk right out loud. Janet spoke even louder as she kept shushing him.

I had a feeling I was going to lose my bet with Jack, and that all forty kids would have to run over my back before I'd wake up enough to take them to the bathroom. It seemed like an effort to pull off my shoes and unzip my bag. Unbraiding my hair took forever. I didn't hear any movement next to me and turned sideways to see what Jack was doing. Watching me unbraid my hair.

"Is something wrong?" I asked.

"No." He smiled and laid down on his bag, which was about a foot from mine.

I combed through my hair, then laid down quickly on my stomach, turning my head away from him.

"If I can't see your eyes, how am I going to be sure you're still awake?" he asked.

"You win. I'll buy dinner. Good night."

"Carly, are you mad at me?"

"I'm just very tired, okay?" My voice wavered.

"Okay," he said. He reached over and gave my sleeping bag a light tug, not touching me, just the bag. "Don't worry about the kids. I'll handle them. Sleep tight."

I don't remember hearing the kids quiet down completely. I heard summer sounds and the kids' whispers, then everything got kind of wavy, voices sounding like they were on a tape that hadn't been wound right. Faces—ghosts of people I knew—floated in front of my eyes. My mom and dad dressed in their airplane clothes, my sister in a little girl's jumper she'd worn back in grade school, a baby in a blanket. I couldn't see the baby's face.

"Buddy," I said quietly. "Buddy, listen. It's going to be all right. You don't need a dad. I'm going to teach you how to throw and catch. Aunt Carly will be there every game."

Then Heather stood beside me. She turned to me, her large gray eyes filling with tears.

"What?" I asked. "What is it, Heather?"

Her face faded, and I must have fallen into a deeper sleep, but some time later, all the faces came back again.

Heather's eyes were shining with tears.

"I'm sorry, Carly, I'm really sorry," she said.

I turned around to see where we were. A cavernous place with a basketball net at one end of the building and a crucifix at another. Everyone was dressed in black. It was a funeral. My mother, father, and I were standing in a pew. My mother, father, and I.

"Joelle? Joe?"

I looked down at the casket. The truth dawned slowly. Joelle and Buddy were in there. I couldn't breathe. I felt as if someone had taken a knife and ripped out the center of me.

It couldn't be true—every part of me said this couldn't be true. But Heather was weeping next to me.

"Joelle? Joelle, is it you? Joe!" I cried out. "No!"

"Carly. Carly, hush. Everything's okay."

I felt a hand over my mouth, and another on my shoulder. Jack was leaning over me, shaking me awake. "Everything's okay."

"Oh, no."

"It was just a dream," he said.

I was shaking all over. The casket was so real. The sense of Joelle's presence inside it was more real than Jack or my sleeping bag or the night around us. I

135

stared up at him but kept sinking back into the images from the dream.

Jack pulled me up into a sitting position. "Come on now, wake up."

His arms wrapped around me and held me up.

"You're okay," he whispered.

I shook my head.

"Yes, you are," he said. His face was against mine and I could feel the words spoken on my cheek.

"She—she's not okay." I could barely get it out. "Joelle's not."

"Joelle is home with your parents," he said gently, firmly. "It was a dream."

But I could not stop shaking. "Dreams mean things."

He stroked my face. "Sometimes," he said, "all they mean is that we're scared."

I hid my face in Jack's chest and began to cry. He held on to me tightly. I started sobbing, and he rocked me slowly back and forth.

What if the dream was prophetic? What if I lost Joelle? A huge part of my life would be gone that could never be replaced.

"I thought . . . she was dead," I said. The heaves were becoming hiccups. Still he held me tight. My nose was running like crazy.

"I need a tissue," I told him, groping with a free hand.

Still holding on to me, he reached for my backpack. Maybe he knew, if he'd let go I would have crumpled on the ground.

"I can't deal with her, Jack. When she didn't listen to the doctor, I started yelling at her, telling her she'd make a terrible mother. All along I've said things that upset her. I've been awful."

"Maybe you haven't been a saint," he said. "But it's a tough situation. Joelle hasn't dealt with it perfectly, has she? She's made a few mistakes. Why can't you?"

"Because I'm the strong one," I said quickly.

His hand brushed my mouth, and I lowered my voice, glancing over at the kids. They were sleeping like kittens.

"I've always been the tough one," I told him quietly. "I'm supposed to be there for her. And I'm not supposed to be thinking all kinds of selfish things."

"I think you are there for her in ways that you don't realize," he replied. With one hand he rubbed my back in slow, soothing circles. "From the little I've seen of Joelle, I'd say she's pretty sharp. I think she came home from college and has stayed close to you because she figured out long ago that you're there for her—much more than you know."

"Maybe," I said and reached into my backpack. There were only three tissues left in my plastic pack. I pulled away from him and started searching the bag.

"I could rip off my shirt and make a nose tourniquet," Jack suggested.

I laughed, then he gave me a wad from his own pack.

When I finally finished blowing, I lay down on my sleeping bag. I was afraid to close my eyes. "What if the dream comes back and I wake you up again?"

"That's okay," he said gently.

"What if it happens all night?"

"About four o'clock, I'll ask Hau to switch places with me." He laid down and smiled at me.

I closed my eyes, trying to hold onto the image of him lying beside me, trying to keep that feeling that everything would turn out all right for Joelle and Buddy and me. We were silent for a while. I listened to Jack's even breathing and thought he was asleep. A tear from nowhere slipped down my cheek.

Jack reached across and took my hand. He squeezed it hard. I don't know how long he held onto it, because a few minutes later I was sound asleep.

FOURTEEN

B Y SATURDAY AFTERNOON, it looked as if the entire
house had been stuffed into one bedroom. Joelle
was allowed up and down the steps twice a day, but with
everything she could possibly want around the perime-
ter of her bed, she spent a lot of time in our room.

"Why don't we just bring up the microwave and
toaster oven?" I said to my father.

"Well, Kitten, that's an idea. Maybe the microwave."

I slammed my hand against my forehead and
walked away.

And now I was adding to the mess, having pulled
out four pairs of shorts, three tops, several pairs of
shoes, and boxes of earrings and hair ribbons. I stood
in front of the mirror and yanked my hair up, then
pulled it down.

"What are you trying to decide?" Joelle asked, as if
she didn't know. Twice she had asked me what time
Jack was coming.

But I answered nicely; I was turning over a new leaf. "Which pair of shorts to wear, which shirt, which shoes, and whether or not to braid my hair."

"In other words," she remarked, "whether or not to try for him."

"That's not what I said, Joelle."

"Do you have the guts to?" she asked.

I began to brush my hair.

"Do you have the nerve to risk it one more time?"

I brushed hard.

"Why don't you give old Heather a run for her money?" she persisted.

"How many times do I have to explain?" I said. "Jack has asked me to help him win her. That's the whole purpose of tonight's date."

"Okay, okay, chill out."

I brushed my hair furiously.

"Carly, stop!" she cried, catching my hand. "You're going to make yourself bald."

I sat down on the bed, my scalp tingling, looking at my choices of clothes.

"I'll make it easy for you," Joelle said. "I'll do your hair and pick out your clothes. Come on—I'd like to. There's no point in fixing myself up anymore."

"Joe, that's not—"

She laughed away my protest. "Be a good kid. Give me something to do. It will be like when we were little and played hair salon."

"Maybe another time," I said, then saw the look on her face. She was bored out of her mind. "Okay, Miss Emerald." That was the name she always chose.

That afternoon, Miss Emerald outdid herself. "Casual but elegant," she said. She pulled my hair up in a soft knot on top of my head, so that I looked like one of those romantic women in an ad from 1910, then she picked out simple drop earrings. She lent me a cotton blouse she still hadn't worn for the first time. It was fitted, giving me a really good figure—a totally different look from my usual big T-shirt style. She insisted I wear a short skirt; I finally agreed to shorts that were dressier than my usual gym type. She did my makeup, and when it was all over, though I was dressed for a baseball game, I looked as good as I did on prom night.

We went downstairs, and my father walked past me, then turned back to look. "Well, you look very nice, K—"

"Don't call me Kitten!"

It had taken me thirteen years to work up the nerve, but I'd finally said it.

My father seemed taken aback for a moment, then gave a little nod and escaped into the kitchen. "Is it her period?" I heard him ask my mother.

Then the doorbell rang. My parents came out briefly for the formalities. Joelle was unusually pleasant, responding to each of Jack's questions and comments with full sentences and an encouraging smile. At last we were off.

"We'll grab a quick dinner at one of the pubs close to the park," Jack said, "then walk over to the game."

"Messina's pitching," I told him. "And Randy Johnson, the Orioles' nemesis. Should be a great game." I started in on comfortable baseball talk and chattered for most of the drive into the city, afraid of having a long silence between us, or worse, a conversation about Heather. Twenty-five minutes later, when I had run out of fascinating things to say about our pitching rotation,

Jack turned into a downtown parking garage.

"What's different about you tonight?" he asked as we stepped onto the garage elevator.

I looked down at myself. "Joelle was bored. She dressed me, fixed my hair and all."

"How's it going with her?"

"Better." The elevator floor suddenly dropped beneath us. I reached for the railing, but Jack caught my arm. "It's . . . um . . . better just having my parents home and not being the responsible one."

"You look nice," he told me.

Nice.

Well, nice was nice. The fact was, this was as good as it got with me—minus sequins—but how could he rate it much higher than "nice" when he was pursuing the likes of Heather.

"Thanks," I said. "You look nice too."

He laughed out loud.

We ate at Balls, which was jam-packed with people gulping down skins and burgers and crab cakes, talking and laughing with one eye up on ESPN, the other following Game of the Week. It was a far cry from Rita's Health Bar & Buy.

I studied the menu, changing my mind several times, then looked up at Jack.

"What are you staring at?" I asked.

"Same thing the jock across the room is staring at."

I turned around and met the guy's eyes. The corner of his mouth drew up in a flirty smile, then he turned back to his buddies.

I blushed, and Jack laughed low in his throat, moving his hand so that it very naturally grazed mine.

"Should you be doing that?" I asked.

"Doing what?"

Immediately I felt silly. It was probably accidental. Then his hand grazed mine again.

"That."

"I thought I was supposed to be practicing. After all, the last time we went out on a date—"

"It wasn't a date," I corrected him. "It was just a group of people having a good time together."

"Right," he said, grinning. "And you were giving me lots of advice. I figured I must be a real amateur. This is my chance to practice with the pro, so I'm practicing. Is that okay?"

"Sure. Fine. I'm ready to order." I waved to the waitress.

Despite what I'd said, every time Jack practiced his flirting, I waved to the waitress. After several rounds of appetizers and sodas, the woman must have figured I was in charge. The check got left with me.

Jack reached over and picked it up.

"I'm paying. I fell asleep first," I reminded him, taking it back.

"I know, but I owe you," he said, putting his hand on mine. "Look how you've helped me with Heather."

"Look how you helped me with Luke."

We stared at each other for a moment, then split the bill and left.

"Are you sure you don't want me to explain anything to Luke?" Jack asked as we waited to cross the street to the ballpark.

He was studying my face. I wondered if he suspected that Luke was no longer in the picture.

"Thanks, but I took care of it. Light's turned," I said and was the first one off the curb.

I love the hustle and bustle of the crowd around the ballpark—the peanut sellers, the guys barking game programs, the booths with pennants flying. Inside Camden Yards, I love going by Boog's Barbecue, taking deep breaths of the steamy, spicy stuff. Jack reached for my hand as I rushed ahead. I just about dragged him up the ramp, higher and higher, hurrying toward section 312.

There's nothing like climbing the ramps, hearing the crowd noise building around you, and finally emerging high in the air, with the brilliant green field and its perfectly cut diamond far beneath you. It made me breathless.

"When I was a kid," I told Jack, "I dreamed of being two things, a princess and an Oriole outfielder."

The way he smiled into my eyes sent me higher than the stadium lights.

"What do you dream about now?" he asked.

I glanced away, then sat down. "Nothing really. Nothing good." I didn't allow myself to daydream at all anymore, not about guys, not about college. Why set myself up for disappointment? As for what I dreamed at night, he already knew about that.

Jack put his arm around my shoulders.

"Practicing again," I said.

"No," he replied. "Just being a friend."

He gave me a pat, then pulled his arm away and started reading the giant scoreboard.

We stood up for the "National Anthem," Jack singing out while I croaked along, then settled into our seats again to watch a fantastic pitching duel. It was the nicest feeling, just being there with Jack, cracking peanuts with him, watching the game, watching the crowd. We talked baseball and the kids. We talked a little about Joelle, and then about sketches Jack was working on at home, and his school back in Pennsylvania. It felt like he was my oldest friend in the world.

Inning after inning flew by, then we stood up for the seventh-inning stretch. Jack turned and said, "Where's the best spot to kiss a girl?"

I blinked. "You mean, other than her lips?"

Jack burst out laughing. "I meant the best *place,* the most romantic—on top of a hill, by the water, in the middle of an intersection?"

"Oh."

His eyes were still glistening. "But answer *your* question," he said, obviously amused.

Instead I started singing and stomping my feet to "Thank God I'm a Country Boy," which was blaring out over the PA system.

"Tell me where," he said at the end of the song.

"The neck."

"Why?"

A very large woman in stretchy orange pants and a Cal Ripkin T-shirt turned her head toward us. I guess she also wanted to hear why.

"I don't know. I suppose a kiss on the forehead means you're a little girl. A kiss on the cheek is for relatives and politicians. A kiss on the hand is charming, you know, old-fashioned and sort of royal. But on the neck—that's something else, maybe because your neck is a very vulnerable spot."

He stared at mine and I put my hand over it.

"Okay," he said, "How about place?" he asked. "What's the most romantic place?"

"Heather would say anywhere close to the water. Her swimming pool, or the harbor, even a fountain."

"And what would you say?"

I reached under my chair for my soda, then stood up again, sucking long and hard on the straw. "I'm not a good person to ask. And if I were you, I wouldn't pay any attention to my neck theory. I'm not as sure about things as I once was."

"You mean you're no longer the guru of dating?" He was mocking me. "You're not the expert on how to catch a girl or guy?"

"Guess not."

"When did you decide this?" he asked curiously.

"Not soon enough," I said.

"Down in front," a fan behind us yelled, and I was glad to drop down in my seat and focus on the game.

Fortunately, both pitchers lost it that inning, and the bull pens were miserable, so we were kept busy watching eleven runs cross the plate. The Orioles won with a homer in the ninth.

"Well, that was great," I told Jack when we emerged from the stadium. "Thanks. Now if we can just find the car again."

"I'd like to walk over to the harbor," he said.

I must have looked as reluctant as I felt.

"Come on, Carly, what are we going to tell Heather?" he asked. "I mean, that's the whole point of tonight, isn't it?"

"Of course," I said.

"Well, I don't think a baseball game is high up on Heather's list of terrific dates."

I knew it wasn't.

"But a long walk—close to the water, as you said—"

"Okay, okay, sure."

"Did Heather say anything to you about us going out tonight?" he asked me as we crossed bridges between buildings on the way to the harbor.

"No. I haven't heard from her since Tuesday. I guess she's mad."

The strange thing was, I didn't care. I was relieved not to see the light blinking on my answering machine and hear her saying how much she needed to talk to me about Jack, Dancing Dan, whoever.

When Jack and I reached Harborplace, we followed the brick pathway around to the aquarium and watched the seals for a while. Then we circled back past the shops and open cafés, the colorful carousel and darkened Rash Field. I had been there many times before, but it all seemed different tonight. We walked quietly and stopped at the southern bank of the harbor, looking across the water at the city. Its tall buildings were rectangles of winking light, with a huge silver moon floating above them. Boats bobbed in the harbor and soft, summertime voices carried over the water. A line of buoys sequined the dark mouth of the inlet with red and green lights.

Neither Jack nor I said anything, but I wondered how it made him feel, if it made music in his head, or shaped itself into pictures to be sketched. I became aware of him standing behind me and instinctively turned my head toward him. He was standing very close, almost touching me. He lowered his head, his cheek almost brushing mine, his mouth an inch from my mouth. His lips moved closer. He was a breath away.

"You're practicing," I said.

"Right. That's right. How'm I doing, Coach, even if you're not an expert anymore?"

"I think you're ready for the big leagues," I replied, breaking away from him. "And I'm ready to go home."

He looked surprised. "You want to leave?"

"Yup."

Jack looked at me puzzled, his hands hanging by his sides. He shoved them into his pockets. "All right," he said.

We retraced our steps, and I noticed that the city was not sparkling as much as I had thought. An ugly theory had begun to form in my mind. Jack wasn't really a nice guy. He wasn't simply seeking my help to win Heather; he was playing a double game—one with her, one with me—and enjoying every minute of it. Maybe he knew I was getting hooked. Maybe he was doing all he could do to draw me in, a kind of revenge for all the times I had looked right past him. It hurt terribly to think that.

Well, grow up, I told myself. *It hurts Joelle to think that the father of her baby isn't a real nice guy.*

It was a long ride home. About two blocks from my house, we rode down a narrow avenue that was a tunnel of shade trees.

Jack slowed down to a crawl. "I haven't searched out the dark streets yet," he said.

"Well, after you've dropped me off, drive around," I told him.

He glanced sideways at me, then picked up speed. Finally, we were home. I got out of the car before Jack did, but he caught up with me on the path.

For the last two years I've been complaining about the way my parents keep the house floodlights on

148

when I'm out on a date. Every time a guy kisses me good night, I expect a director to yell "cut." But tonight I was grateful.

"I guess your parents want to make sure you get safely inside the door," Jack remarked, glancing up at the lights.

"Yeah, and when we're out here squinting at each other, it's a lot easier for my father to watch every move from the dark house without being seen."

It was a lie, but it gave me one last shot of courage to finish off what I had started. "Good night," I said cheerfully, and stood on tiptoe to kiss him on the cheek—far away from his mouth—just about on his ear. Then the lights went out.

All of them—the porch light, the floodlights, the light at the end of the walk. I froze, caught off balance, tottering too close to him in the darkness. His arms went around me, then he pulled me against him. He was going to kiss me. And I couldn't think of one smart comment to stop him. Even worse, I didn't want to think of one smart comment.

He slowly bent his head, but his mouth didn't touch mine. I figured he had changed his mind. Then I felt his lips against my neck. On my throat I felt a long, warm, soft-as-a-summer-night kiss.

"See you, Carly," he said, and left me on the doorstep trembling.

FIFTEEN

I FELT LIKE 7.5 on the Richter scale, but I guess it was just my knees. The house was still standing and the leaves on our old maple barely stirred.

My trembling hands wouldn't work the house key—I may as well have been using a fork—then I discovered that the front door was already unlocked. I saw Jack pause by his car, making sure I could get in. Well, he'd have plenty to tell Heather now. She'd be rushing into his arms just as he planned—just as *we* planned.

I pushed open the door.

"Hope I cut the lights at the right time," Joelle said.

She was sitting at the top of the stairs in her nightgown.

I turned on the hall lamp. "Perfect." My voice was flat. I had gone from quaking to completely numb inside. I climbed the steps slowly.

"You okay?" Joelle asked.

"Sure."

Stepping around her, I headed for the bathroom before she asked too many questions. I washed my face with the medicine-cabinet door open so I wouldn't have to watch the perfect makeup job turn back into an ordinary-looking face. All I wanted to do was climb into bed and pull the sheets over my head and sleep. But when I walked into our bedroom, I saw a pan of brownies and glass of water waiting for me on the table between our beds.

"I can't do any more stairs today, so if you want milk, you'll have to get it yourself," Joelle said from her canyon of pillows.

I really wasn't hungry, but she had gone to some trouble to make the brownies for me. Just one square was missing from the pan, which meant she had even fended off my father.

"They look great," I said, trying to sound enthusiastic as I cut into them.

"Carly, I'm sorry it didn't work out tonight the way you wanted it to."

I shrugged. "I knew it would end up like this. I knew what I was getting myself into, but I owed him." I poked the knife at some crumbs. "Though it wasn't just that," I said quietly. "I know this sounds crazy, but I really do want Jack to be happy—even if being happy means being with Heather. So I helped him along. Crazy, huh?"

"Craziness runs in the family," Joelle said, throwing one leg over the side of the bed. "But listen, you may be surprised. I wish it was Jack who'd surprise you—but if he doesn't, somebody else will. It's true," she said, swinging her foot.

"Carly, if there is one thing I've learned in the last

couple of weeks, it's that people are full of surprises. They have little ways of being there for you, of making you smile when you've decided you won't ever again. And that gets you through," she said, glancing up at the shelf that held Harry's bears and the kids' cards.

I chewed thoughtfully.

"Other people will get you through," she repeated. "Trust me on that."

I wasn't going to commit myself. "Aren't you having any brownies?"

"Already did. Dad and I split that square."

"Yeah, but you're eating for two, Joe. You've got to get serious about this if Buddy is going to be born a chocoholic—which I'm counting on. I'm planning to buy humongous chocolate bunnies each Easter, which Buddy will gratefully share with Aunt Carly. And when Buddy can walk, we're dressing up and going trick-or-treating together, a shopping bag in each of Buddy's hands. Then at Christmas, well, let's just say I have big plans for chocolate bonding with this kid."

Joelle laughed and cut us each a brownie. We ate in silence, but it was a comfortable one, and she was still smiling a little. Then we turned off the light.

The ache wasn't gone. When I closed my eyes, I imagined Heather lounging by the pool talking to Jack on her pink cordless phone, while he hurried around his room, packing his swim shorts and towel. If anything, the pain had rooted deeper.

But the little surprises were there too. The brownies. Joelle smiling.

Tomorrow I'd find ways of keeping busy—maybe I'd paint the old bureau that was going to be Buddy's. And come Monday, there'd be a busful of noisy kids who'd be full of surprises. That would get me through.

"It's hard to understand why Aunt Madeleine would paint a bureau passion purple," I said, glancing down at my arms. The sanded-off paint had mixed with sweat and was turning my skin a shiny violet. "Wasn't she in the convent once?"

"Maybe that's why," Joelle replied. She reclined in a shady lounge chair about ten feet away from where I was working in the backyard. Lying in her lap was an anthropology book I had slipped into her stack of magazines. She was just thumbing through it, looking at the pictures, but it was a start.

Strange as it sounds, I was glad for Joelle's company as I sanded away my frustrations. The Sunday afternoon sun burned a hot yellow circle around our tree. I stood back now, wiping the perspiration from my brow, admiring the ultrasmooth surface of the bureau's top and sides.

"Hello, Heather," Joelle said.

I turned around. This was not the kind of surprise I had hoped for.

She looked so pretty. How come she always looked pretty? How come I never caught her in a sweaty, holey T-shirt and uneven cutoffs, wearing a messy braid, with freckles and purple dust all over her?

"Heather, what's up?" I asked, wondering if she noticed the false cheerfulness in my voice. "I haven't seen you for a while."

"You haven't called me for a while," she replied. I heard the hurt in her voice—real or unreal, I wasn't sure.

"Grab a chair from the porch," I told her.

While she went to get one, Joelle asked quietly, "Want me to leave?"

"No." It came out sounding angry. Actually, I was panicked. I wanted my older sister's sarcasm around as a kind of shield.

"What's the bureau for?" Heather asked, pulling her chair up halfway between me and Joelle.

"The baby. I'm going to paint it yellow, and do some trim later on when we find out whether Buddy's a boy or girl."

"How are you feeling, Joelle?" Heather asked. "Any better?"

"Aglow with womanhood," Joelle replied.

Heather nodded seriously. I snorted, and got paint dust up my nose.

"I guess it's been busy lately," Heather said softly, "maybe with the baby coming and all."

I began to feel guilty. I should have made an effort to call her.

"Sure keeps me busy," Joelle replied, "sitting still all day."

"We used to talk every day, Carly," Heather continued, "and see each other every weekend."

I nodded. "Yeah. I guess things have been a little different lately." I began sanding one of the drawers.

"I suppose you've been going out a lot," Heather said.

I glanced up at her. "Some."

"When Jack and I decided to date other people—though we're still seeing each other, of course," she added quickly, "he told me he was asking you out."

I kept sanding.

"I was—well—really surprised."

"Why?" asked Joelle. "It made a lot of sense to me."

Heather glanced at Joelle and pulled her chair closer to me. "It used to be we couldn't wait to tell each other about our dates. How was last night? Did you have a good time?" she asked.

"Yeah. I did. Did you have a good time with . . . uh . . . Dan?"

"It was okay. He has a girlfriend, you know. He's been going with her for a long time."

"At least three years, I remember," I said, and went after a sharp corner of the drawer.

"Dan's really nice," Heather continued. "We're terrific together—when we dance. But that's pretty much it, I think."

"Oh." If only I had Mount Rushmore to sand, all four heads of the presidents, then I'd have something equal to my energy.

Heather shrugged her shoulders and smiled. "Maybe I'm glad. Maybe it's time that I stop falling for guys that belong to other girls."

Joelle rolled her eyes.

"Pretty amazing, isn't it?" Heather went on. "This gorgeous guy walks into my life, completely unattached, and I fall for him."

"I guess you're not the first person it's happened to," I said.

"What do you mean by that?" A worry line creased her forehead.

"Well—well, you saw all the girls at Steve's party," I replied quickly. "They were crazy about him."

"Then I guess I'm pretty lucky," she said. "Jack's mine. He's mine, Carly."

I kept quiet. A huge lump—maybe it was a tumor of purple paint dust—formed in my throat.

"Have you told Jack that?" Joelle asked loudly. Much too loudly, I thought.

"Told Jack what?" he echoed.

Apparently my sister had seen him coming around the side of the house. He strode across the lawn smiling at us. I was dumbfounded. Why had he come? Why hadn't he told me he was stopping by? I looked a mess, especially next to Heather.

"Well, I guess you're not quite ready, Carly," he said.

Ready? I thought. "No, after this we've got to do Buddy's crib."

He laughed. "I meant ready for me." He looked at me meaningfully. "Did you forget?"

I turned to Joelle, who was laughing behind her book. Big help.

"Did you forget our date?"

I squinted at him, then glanced down at my sweaty purple arms and legs—I looked like an escapee from a tropical fish tank.

"We were going to the zoo," Jack said.

"The zoo!"

Heather was looking back and forth between us, her beautiful mouth a long, straight line. If it began to tremble, the way it always did before she cried, I'd be mush. But then, Jack would be mush too, and he would turn to her tenderly and carry her off and this whole miserable charade would be over. He was pushing his luck, playing the game this hard. If he kept it up, he'd have two bawling girls on his hands.

I looked him straight in the eye, which took about

156

all my courage. "You've made a mistake," I said firmly. "A *big* mistake."

He blinked. The expression on his face was unreadable, but I could tell that he suddenly wasn't so sure of himself. He scowled. I scowled back. Heather, of course, was busy with a pretty pout.

"I guess this is what happens when you play the field," I said. "You can't remember who you've got a date with and when. Dan's probably home wondering why Heather hasn't shown up yet. Meanwhile, Jack, you're at the wrong house."

Nobody, including me, believed what I was saying. The truth was I hadn't the faintest idea why Jack had come to see me—unless Mrs. Larsson had told him that Heather was headed this way, and he thought he'd score a few more points. I really hated this game.

Heather continued to pout.

Oh, suck it in, I wanted to say to her. You've won.

"Brownies, anyone?" Joelle asked.

"Yeah," said Jack.

I watched him eat three.

Heather picked crumbs out of the pan, licking them delicately off her fingers, then said casually, "That was a great game you two saw."

I stared at her. She had never shown any interest in the Orioles.

"Two of the best pitchers in the National League," she went on.

American, I silently corrected her.

"What a pitching duo!"

Duel, I thought. She must have heard the term on a sports report.

"The eighth inning was really exciting," she

157

continued. "How about that play at the plate?"

I almost laughed. Next she'd be slapping us on the back and saying, "How about them Os!"

"I never thought they'd try a suicide squish!"

"You mean *suicide squeeze*," Joelle corrected her.

Heather nodded, then ran down a list of baseball observations she must have picked up from the newspaper or TV. Figuring these tidbits were bait to get us talking about last night's date, I ignored them and started sanding the second drawer. Jack tried to change the subject. He probably wanted to tell her the romantic parts of our date when I wasn't around, elaborating on them a bit. Or maybe he was just too busy stuffing his mouth with brownies.

When I got tired of it all, I said, "Well, you guys are wasting a great afternoon."

"I guess so," Jack muttered, looking really annoyed at me. "So, Heather, do you want to go in your car or mine?"

"If we're going to the zoo, I have to go home and change my shoes," she replied.

"Okay. I'll follow you."

And they were gone, except that Jack turned back for a moment and shot me a look that went through me like a steel blue shaft.

I met his eyes as steadily as possible. "I was wrong about you," I said softly. "You know exactly what you're doing."

He opened his mouth as if he were going to reply, then swiped another brownie and left.

SIXTEEN

IT WASN'T HARD to avoid Jack Monday morning, because he was busy avoiding me. But as luck would have it, it was our day for lunch duty together. I wondered if he had told Anna what was going on, or if she instinctively circulated in the territory between the two of us. I thought we were hiding the tension between us really well, then Eugene asked, "You and Mr. Jack fighting?"

Eugene asked the question the way he always asked something—loudly—and Jack heard it. He came over quickly. "Miss Carly is my friend," he said. "We're busy working now, but when we're not, we talk a lot and have a good time. We like a lot of the same things."

Like Heather, I thought.

"We went to see an Orioles game this weekend," Jack told him, resting his hand on my back.

"Yeah, it was fun," I said.

We stood side by side, smiling at Eugene, as if we were posing for a yearbook photo. Then

159

Heather walked in. She came straight toward us.

"Who's the babe?" Eugene asked, knowing it was a question that usually got a reaction.

"She's my friend Heather," I replied. "I'd like you to show her respect and not call her anything other than her real name," I added. But I thought to myself—*you've got that right, kid.*

She was wearing one of her leotard-skirt outfits, going to dance class, I guessed. Only I had never seen this leotard. And I had watched her try on every leotard she ever owned, and at least six hundred others she didn't. It may seem like a small, unimportant fact, but it signaled to me how much things had changed between us.

"Hi, Carly. Hi, Jack." Her voice kind of melted when she spoke Jack's name. Eugene eyed her, then glanced at me.

She hooked onto Jack, and we stood there for a moment like the Three Musketeers. Jack slowly lifted his hand from my back.

"I just ran into Harry," she said to Jack. "He's having old friends and camp guys over tomorrow for the Fourth of July."

Camp guys—those are my guys, not yours, I thought. *Don't talk about Harry and the other counselors as if they're your pals.*

"I told him we didn't have plans yet," she continued, "and answered yes for both of us."

We. Both of us. I moved away from the happy couple.

April, my barrette girl, reached out a peanut-buttery hand. "Know where I'm going Fourth of July?"

"Where?" I asked.

"To the parade. The one they have around here. My aunt's bringing me on the bus."

"Really! Aunts are pretty cool, aren't they?" I said, and made up my mind that Joelle and I would hit all the big Independence Day sales and come home loaded with stuff for Buddy.

At the end of lunch, when Harry called me over, I had my excuse for tomorrow evening all ready. Harry looked terribly disappointed.

"I guess it's better not to ask Joelle then," he said. "She probably wouldn't want to come without you."

"Well, you never know." Getting out would be good for Joelle, I thought, and Harry would watch out for her. "Why don't you call and ask her?"

"Would you ask her for me?" he replied. "Tell her it's a frat house, but I'm the only one there this summer, and there's a bathroom on the first floor, which will be clean by then, and just two steps into the house, and lots of old chairs to sit on, and I'll fix her whatever she likes to eat."

"I'll tell her."

I did later that afternoon while she was stirring spaghetti sauce and I was washing veggies.

"What time are people getting there?" Joelle asked.

I was surprised that she didn't immediately reject the idea. "Six o'clock. Harry said you'll be able to see some of the local fireworks from his yard."

She stirred a couple more times, then I saw her steal a sideways glance at herself in the toaster mirror. "What are you wearing?" she asked.

"I'm not going."

"What? Why would I go if you're not?"

"To have a good time," I said.

161

"But I won't know anybody there."

"You'll know Harry and Jack," I reminded her. "And Heather."

"Oh," she replied with an all-knowing voice. "That's why you're staying home. You're going to mope."

"I'm not moping."

"And I'm not going, unless you do."

So I called Harry and told him I had wiggled out of "the other party" and asked him what Joelle and I could bring to his.

"Some dessert," he said. "Brownies. Anything chocolate. I've really been craving chocolate lately."

It's becoming an epidemic, I thought.

The next day Joelle and I showed up along with an army of college-age kids. I should have guessed that Harry would have a zillion friends. The old wooden frat house with its sagging banner and sagging porch and patched-up roof was off campus. It had a large yard where it looked to me as if Harry had spent the day trimming weeds into lumps resembling bushes. A collection of rickety garage-sale chairs were spread around for anyone who dared to try one; Harry had set aside one sturdy chair for Joelle. When he saw us enter the backyard, his whole face brightened.

We were the first "campers" to arrive, he told us, then introduced us to friends of his. I was glad to have a chance to mix in before Jack and Heather came. Harry brought over a guy who was an anthropology major to talk to Joelle, and found for me two friends who played varsity sports at Kirbysmith. He was being just good old Harry, laughing and waving his arms as he moved around the crowd, but it was no different than camp: He always had one eye out for others, trying to make it easier for them however he could.

Anna arrived a little later with a gorgeous guy on her arm, then Hau showed up alone. Pamela walked in with two giggling girlfriends. I began to hope that Jack and Heather had found something better to do, but they got there as the first batch of hamburgers was coming off the grill.

Anna saw them first and pointed them out to her boyfriend, Chuku. We all looked up at the same time.

"Well, not much chance of Jack drifting off to sea," Joelle observed. "Not the way Heather's got him anchored."

"Maybe it's Jack's hand that's doing the anchoring," I suggested.

Anna put up her arm, which was a long swirl of bracelets. "I doubt it," she said, and waved Jack over.

Jack saw us and turned Heather in our direction. "Hey, guys!"

The two of them joined our crowd, and for the first twenty minutes Jack talked and joked and looked at everyone but me. Heather stood close to him. She was attracting lots of glances from guys outside our circle. *What a rush it must be for him,* I thought, *to bring a girl to a party and have all the guys stare at her.* Then I caught Jack staring at my hair, which I had left down that night. The weather was humid and I figured it was expanding into its electrified look.

Heather was explaining ballet moves to Anna, giving a little demonstration. Jack moved closer to Joelle and me.

"When your hair looks like—like that—it's not ironed, is it?" Jack asked.

163

"Of course not," I replied. "I just ran a garden rake through it."

One side of his mouth drew up.

"How was the zoo?" I asked.

"Good. Fun. I'm really sorry you didn't come."

"You know, Jack, sometimes you can play a game too hard."

"Which game?" he asked.

"Oh, give me a break!" I cried angrily.

Jack turned away, and after that we managed to keep everybody in our group between the two of us. I didn't glance in his direction again until the fireworks.

People had spread old sheets and blankets on the front lawn, facing away from the house. I had found a seat on the porch steps. Joelle left the others to join me.

"Having a good time?" I asked. But I could see the answer to my question in the high color in her cheeks. For a few hours, at least, she had turned back into a nineteen-year-old college student.

"Yeah, I really am. How about you?"

"It hasn't been too bad," I said with shrug, "Oh, look!"

She glanced up at the sky and we oohed and aahed together at the first burst and shimmer of color, then at each glittering explosion that followed.

"I like the green."

"The purple."

"The blue and pink together."

"Oh, the fish! Your favorite, Carly—the hissing fish!"

But I had begun watching a different set of fireworks.

164

Heather and Jack were sitting on a blanket together. She wrapped an arm around him and, with her other hand, turned his face slowly toward her. He bent his head, looking at her. He gazed at her for what seemed like an eternity. *He's going to kiss her,* I thought, *he's going to kiss her on the neck the same way he kissed me.* Of course, I was the one who had advised him to.

But he went for the mouth. I felt my own go soft. They kissed and kissed. I could not stop staring at the spot where his lips touched hers. That small, indefinable ache had become so intense I felt as if I couldn't breathe.

"Keep your eyes on the sky," Joelle said.

"I can't."

"Don't make it more than it is, Carly. Remember, she started it."

"He's finishing it," I said. "I wish I were home."

"Soon. When the fireworks are over."

Then Joelle did a funny thing: she was sitting on the step below me and reached across and put a hand around my ankle. Our family is not the touching type. Joelle and I hadn't hugged or held hands since we were little girls in a spook house. I guess that's why she didn't really know what to do and decided to hold onto my ankle. Tears were burning behind my eyes, but I almost laughed.

"Hang in there," she said. "I think this is the finale."

In more ways than one, I thought. As soon as the house lights went back on, we found Harry, thanked him, and cut out of there.

SEVENTEEN

"Is it time to get up?" I asked hours later, groping in the dark for my clock. "Is it raining out?"

"It's four o'clock. Go back to sleep," Joelle replied, then padded out of the room.

I rolled over. Five more hours till I had to look like a happy camper. Five more till I had to plaster a smile on my face, telling Jack how glad I was that things had worked out with Heather.

I turned over again and noticed the crack of light. Joelle always sleepwalked to the bathroom in total darkness. But there was a light on now and it stayed on. And on.

I climbed out of bed. "Joelle?"

I tapped on the bathroom door, and when she didn't answer, opened it. She stood there with a towel wrapped around her, shivering and staring at her nightgown in the sink. The faucet dripped, dripped, dripped on the blood.

"It's okay, Joelle," I said. "It's okay. I'll get help."

*　　*　　*

The big window in the hospital waiting room looked east. I had watched the sun come up, then watched the cars turning into the hospital driveway, a few at first, followed by a steady stream just before seven. Breakfast smells rose from the cafeteria making me nauseous, but at eight o'clock I went downstairs with my parents. The three of us sat in plastic chairs, poking at the stuff on our trays, each hoping the others would eat.

My mother reached across the table. "Joelle is going to be all right," she said to me. "She's tough. She's learned how to be tough from you."

We threw away the food and went back upstairs. It was the first time I had ever seen my parents holding hands.

At eight-thirty my father telephoned Harry to say I wasn't coming to work. I couldn't speak to him. I felt as if my voice was down in my stomach.

Later a nurse came for my parents. I stared out the east window some more. I started thinking about Sam. I imagined him saying good morning to his wife, smiling at her, kissing her, and cheerfully heading off to teach a summer course. He had no idea what Joelle was going through. The sun was getting high now.

My father returned and touched me on the arm. "Carly," he said gently, "Joelle wants to see you."

I don't remember who told me, or if anybody did, but I knew before I entered her room that she had miscarried. I knew Buddy was gone.

"Joelle?"

She was propped on pillows with the sheets pulled

167

up under her arms, her face turned toward the window. I didn't know whether to walk around to the other side of the bed or stay where I was, allowing her to keep her face turned away from me.

It was too late to tell her I had planned to teach Buddy to throw and catch. It was too late to say I was going to be Superaunt, and she wouldn't be raising Buddy alone.

"I'm sorry."

She didn't respond.

"I'm sorry about Buddy. . . . And I love you, Joe, for what it's worth."

For a moment, she didn't stir. Then I saw her close her eyes, squeezing them tight.

She turned to me. "Funny thing—it's worth everything."

I put my arms around her and held her. Or maybe Joelle held me. Somehow, between the two of us, we had the strength to sit upright.

"You know," I said a few minutes later, struggling to speak clearly through the tears, "this is looking way too pretty. Let's climb under your hospital bed and throw a temper tantrum."

She opened her mouth as if she would laugh, then sobbed against my shoulder.

At noontime, the doctor released her.

It felt strange to be back in our bedroom, strange that it was just the two of us. Buddy had become a presence even to me; I could hardly imagine what it was like for Joelle having carried the baby.

As soon as she was asleep, I tiptoed over to the bookshelves and moved Harry's mama and baby bear out of sight. I left the kids' cards, so Joelle wouldn't notice what I had done. She slept through the afternoon, while my parents and I took turns staying with her.

Harry called at the end of the camp day. I told him the news. He said the third-graders had made Joelle something and asked whether he should bring it over or wait until I returned to camp. There were only two days of camp left, and I was planning to go to work the next morning, but I told him to come over if he liked. I didn't know if Joelle would want to see him, but I sure wanted to. Even if I couldn't bring myself to talk to him about losing Buddy, Harry's friendly face and steadiness would be a comfort.

He arrived about five-thirty with a scroll of paper that unrolled into a large rectangle, six feet by eight, cracking with thick paint. The kids had created a self-portrait, each one painting his or her own picture in a crowd scene under a circus tent. Some of them had drawn balloons coming out of their mouths and wrote in messages to both Joelle and me. My father picked out Eugene immediately. My mother read the balloons and figured out which one was little brown-nosing Janet. I loved the picture of April, who hadn't bothered painting in all those barrettes but simply globbed her hair with glitter.

"Jack helped them make it," Harry said. "Here's the crib sheet."

I opened up a folded piece of paper on which Jack had made a chart showing the kids' places in the picture. He had slipped in a small piece of paper with a short note: "Is there anything I can do? Call me."

I longed to call him. I longed to have him comfort me. I wanted Jack for just a friend, if that's all it could be—but not now, not yet, I told myself, not until I got over my other feelings for him. I mean, how could we be pals cracking peanuts together, taking in a ball game, when I couldn't stop staring at his lips and imagining what it would be like to kiss him?

I took a deep breath, letting it out slowly. Harry put a hand on my shoulder. My parents were still admiring the painting.

"I'll run upstairs and ask Joelle if she wants a visitor," I told him. "But don't get your feelings hurt, Harry. She probably won't."

"Oh, then I'll say hello another time," he said, pulling out his car keys.

My mother caught him by the arm. "Let Carly ask. Sometimes Joelle surprises us."

She surprised us this time. I directed him upstairs to the second door on the right, then followed my parents into the kitchen. We ate a hodgepodge of leftovers that evening. Every once in a while my mother's eyes would mist up and she'd blink a couple times. I caught my father holding her hand under the table.

Harry stayed for an hour and a half. I wondered what he and Joelle were talking about. I figured as long as she wanted him to stay, he was doing her good.

After Harry left, Mom and I put dinner on a tray for Joelle. Mom's eyes were getting pink again, and I didn't know what to do. "Go on," she said softly, "take the tray up to Joelle. If I can have a good cry over the dishes, I'll feel much better."

I fought back my own tears and picked up the tray. I was halfway up the stairs when the doorbell rang. My father came around behind me to answer it.

"Hello, Heather," he said.

Just what I needed right now—consolation from

Heather. *But she's being nice,* I told myself sternly. *She cares about you.*

"Heather and Luke," my father said. "It's Luke, isn't it?"

I turned around on the steps.

"Jack," he said, and glanced up at me.

"Hi, Heather. Hi, Jack." My mouth felt tight.

"Here, let me take that, Carly," my father offered. "You spend some time with your friends."

After Dad carried off the tray, I joined Jack and Heather at the bottom of the steps. The three of us stood silently in the hall, as comfortable with each other as total strangers at a funeral. The last thing I wanted to do was hang out with them, and I had to wonder how much they wanted to spend date time with me.

Heather was clutching a bouquet wrapped in paper. She rested her other hand on Jack's belt, wrapping a finger around a loop. "We brought Joelle some flowers," she said. "I didn't know her favorite kind, so Jack asked me what yours was. I hope they don't look too ordinary."

"Daisies and baby's breath," I said, avoiding Jack's eyes. "They're beautiful. Joelle will love them. Thanks."

"Harry told us the news this afternoon," Jack said. "I'm really sorry."

I nodded. "Thanks."

"How's she doing?" he asked.

I put my face down in the flowers—as if daisies had a smell. "Physically, she's fine. Other ways, it will probably take a while."

"Is there anything we can do?" Heather asked.

We. Us. They really were a couple now.

"No, but it was great of you to come and bring the flowers." My voice shook.

171

"Oh, Carly, I'm sorry," Heather said. She gave me a warm hug. It was like old times.

I wished it could be old times. I wished Heather and I would always be best friends, wished I was back having silly crushes again, and my heart was still my own. And I wished more than anything that Joelle could be like she was before she'd lost her heart to Sam, then lost it again to his baby.

Heather let go of me. Jack stood still, watching. What was he thinking? I wondered. If only I could touch his hand.

Then Heather leaned back against him, turning her face up to his. "Come on, Jack. Carly looks bushed. I told you we should have called before we came."

She started toward the door.

Jack didn't follow her. He looked at me with eyes that were so intense I felt as if he could read every thought in my mind.

But he can't, I reminded myself. *And it's a good thing.* "Thanks for coming," I said.

Jack nodded slowly.

Heather reached back for him then, and they left, his hand in hers.

I sat on the steps, staring down at the daisies in my lap. I tried to remember the words of one of the lullabies Jack had sung when we stayed overnight at camp. I thought about how he had held me close that night and how, when I thought he was asleep, he had reached out for my hand. In the long run, I was going to be more miserable holding on to such little, meaningless moments. But I was as low as could be right now. And I couldn't give up the comfort of remembering what it was like that one night when Jack reached out to me and didn't let go.

EIGHTEEN

JACK AND I hardly spoke on Thursday, each of us finding ways to be too busy to talk. Now I just had to get through Friday, which was our last day of camp. To celebrate it, Harry had organized a day of games and contests involving all the kids. He had bought bags full of Kmart specials.

"No camper goes home without something," he told us in the morning. We awarded a lot of sixth-, seventh-, and eighth-place winners that day.

At lunchtime, the kids saw their own work mounted by Jack in an art exhibit outside the cafeteria. The artists were bursting with pride, especially when other people from the college stopped and admired their work.

I was standing in front of some of the paintings done by Hau's kids, which showed people and animals with a mix of English and Vietnamese words bubbling out of their mouths. Someone else was looking at them too, standing just behind me. Not Jack—I knew he was keeping his distance, staying on the other side of the exhibit.

"These are terrific, aren't they?" I said, turning around. "Luke!" I exclaimed.

"Hi, Carly." He gazed at me with those soft, sea green eyes.

"How do you like our masterpieces?" I asked him.

"They've got lots of colors," he replied, smiling down at me.

If he ever wins the Olympics, I thought, *he's going to be an advertiser's dream.*

"But some of the colors aren't right," he added. "Like that blue tree."

"I love that blue tree."

"It seems like there are a lot of girls in these pictures with red hair," he went on.

"You noticed that, huh?"

"They make me think of you," he said.

"Really? Thanks."

"There's one with a red-haired girl wearing hearts all over her shirt."

I smiled. "Miguel, my outfielder, painted that. Remember, I told you about him."

"Listen, Carly, I have a meet tomorrow afternoon over at Canton U. It starts at two o'clock. It should be a real good one to watch."

"Then I hope you get a good crowd," I said. "Good luck. I know you'll be great, Luke."

"It starts at two, but you might have things to do," he continued. "My best event isn't till about three-thirty. Come then. I know you'd enjoy it."

"I'm sorry, I do have stuff to do," I replied. "But it was nice of you to ask." I meant it. Luke's idea of a girlfriend was an adoring fan, but his invitation still boosted my ego.

"I—I guess I should have mentioned it earlier," he said, and walked away. About halfway across the lobby he remembered his hero's strut.

When Luke's hunk of a body was no longer blocking my view, I saw that Jack and Anna had been watching us from the other side of the exhibit. I tensed up. *If Jack teases me about Eggbeaters, I'll lose it,* I thought. But Anna said something to him, and he turned away before I did.

At 3:15 the kids lined up for the bus one last time, proudly clutching their prizes and paintings. There were hugs and tearful good-byes. This week seemed to me the week of hard good-byes.

When the bus finally pulled away, the other counselors and I watched and waved. Fifteen feet down the driveway, the bus stopped suddenly and backed up. For a moment everyone wondered what was going on, then the doors opened. Miguel jumped down and ran to me with his painting.

"Here."

"For me? You want me to keep it?" I asked, staring down at the girl wearing hearts all over her shirt.

He nodded, pressing his lips together.

"Terrific. When you're a famous ballplayer, can I bring it to the stadium and get you to sign it?"

Miguel hugged me, then ran back to the bus.

The six of us walked quietly back toward the office. It was cleanup time, and I guess each of us was glad to have something to do while we thought our own thoughts about the kids.

I picked up equipment we had borrowed and carried

it over to the gym. It didn't take long to store the balls and nets in their closets. It was tempting to stay and shoot baskets, waiting for everyone to leave so I could avoid the last set of good-byes. I took out one basketball and dribbled it onto the court. At the foul line, I bounced it several times and set myself for the shot.

"Rebound!"

I turned to look at Jack. "When I shoot, I don't miss."

He raised his eyebrows.

I shot. I missed.

He pulled the rebound off the board and dribbled past me.

"I've got to put that away now," I said, holding out my hand.

"I've got to talk," he replied, dribbling the ball close to me.

"So, stand here and talk if you want. I'm going to put this away." I snatched the ball from him, but he grabbed my arm just as quickly.

"*We've* got to talk."

"I can't think of a good reason why," I said.

"Carly, you look so unhappy. And I don't know what to do to help." The concern on his face was real; it just about broke my heart.

"Please don't do anything," I told him, tracing with my finger a curved line on the basketball. "It's not your problem, Jack." I moved away from him. "Things aren't great right now, it's true, but I set myself up for this."

"No," he replied, "I set us up, when I started playing the Heather game with you."

"*Excuse* me," I retorted. "You may have gotten all

the girls at Steve's party to chase after you, but when it came to you and Heather—get it straight—I'm the one who masterminded that romance."

"You're sure of that," he said, his eyes sparking angrily. "I wonder what makes you so awfully sure *you* are the one calling all the shots—"

"Two points, no rim," I announced, calling my shot, then making it, a clean swish.

Jack retrieved the ball and dribbled it behind the yellow circle. "Three points," he announced, then sunk the ball into the net. He turned to me. "You really don't have a clue about what I've been trying to do."

"I've got a clue all right," I interrupted him. "You're trying to beat me at my own game."

"Which game do you mean, Carly?"

I scooped up the ball.

"Which game?" he insisted.

I twirled around him and went for the left-handed layup. I was furious. I'd lost in love. I wasn't going to be beat shooting baskets.

He caught up with me and made a clean block. We charged after the loose ball, slamming against the wall.

"You know, when I first met you," he said, "that day you almost ran over me, I thought you were a little crazy and should probably always wear your crash helmet."

"Really? How flattering," I said, trying to disentangle my body from his. It made me ache to be so close to him. His voice, his smell, his touch was all around me.

"But, but I guess I was even crazier—"

"I won't argue with that," I snapped, lunging for the ball that was rolling away from us.

177

"—wanting you."

I looked over my shoulder at him. "What did you say?"

"I wanted you. And you wanted Eggbeaters." He laughed. "When I think about it now, it's pretty hilarious."

I was stunned. Why was that funny?

"I got so mad," Jack continued, "when you thought you'd use me to win Eggbeaters. But I agreed to go out with you and Heather, hoping that if you got to know me, you'd change your mind." He looked at me with those incredible blue eyes. "There were a few moments, like in the haunted house, when I thought I had a chance."

Then he shrugged and smiled, as if those moments were no big deal. "You kept coaching me," he went on, "and made it clear you were hot for Eggbeaters. I had to stick it out till Heather got tired of me, so I saw her as much as I could, thinking she'd get bored fast. She did—then I got the brilliant idea." Now the smile disappeared. He shook his head as if he were disgusted with himself.

"What?" I asked hoarsely, "What was the brilliant idea?"

"To try your game—even though I thought it was ridiculous. From the beginning, I hated the way you played your silly dating games. But it seemed so easy! If I pretended that I needed to keep Heather interested, I had an excuse to date you, an excuse you would go along with."

"Oh, jeez."

"Now I feel like a rat. It doesn't matter whether Heather used others—I used her—I am a rat. What feels worse, I fixed it all so perfectly that I couldn't even be a friend to you. Wednesday night, at your house, all I wanted to do was reach for you."

He took a step forward. I picked up the basketball and clutched it like a life preserver. Could he tell I was shaking all over?

"You can let go now," he said quietly. "Game's over."

"Is it?" I whispered. "Who won?"

"Nobody."

"Nobody?"

"Obviously," he snapped. "Not you, not Heather, not me." He turned and walked away.

I stared after him in disbelief. He meant it. It really was over. He had fallen in and out of love with me before I even knew it. It had lasted about as long as a dip in a chilly pool. Now all that was left was anger.

I watched his back for a minute, then took a running start and hurled the ball from half-court toward the basket at the other end of the gym. I wanted to smash the glass backboard into a thousand pieces.

Instead, the ball dropped neatly into the basket.

Jack stopped and waited for the ball to roll back to him. "You know, if you practiced a little," he said, one side of his mouth drawing up, "you'd be sort of a good shot."

"I *am* a good shot."

He nodded toward the basket, then flipped the ball to me, as if he were passing the ball to a teammate. But just after I caught it, he ran over to block my path. I dribbled around him. He stayed with me. I drove hard to the left, then the right. He was with me every step. Pulling back again, I faked and raced for the lane.

I gave him a sneaky elbow in the ribs and took off just beneath the basket. We collided in midair.

"Foul! On the arm," I yelled.

"Are you kidding? Charging!" Jack exclaimed.

We stood there, sweating, looking at each other.

"Carly," he said, his voice so low and breathless I could hardly hear it, "I'm in love with you. It's not over for me. I can't stop being in love with you and I don't know what to do about it."

I swallowed hard. The feelings were so intense, I was terrified. I tried to sound light and breezy. "Apparently, you weren't listening when I gave you all that advice."

He looked amazed, then hopeful, his eyes brightening. "I—I listened to some of it." He put his arms around me loosely, then leaned down and kissed me on the neck—once, twice, three times—delicate butterfly kisses.

He pulled back and looked at me. "You're shivering!"

"Really."

He pulled me against him, his arms encircling me like he'd never let go, then lowered his mouth toward mine.

"Carly, close your eyes."

I closed both, then opened one.

Jack laughed out loud. His mouth felt like a smile on mine and I could feel him laughing all up and down his body. He kissed me gently, gently again, waiting for me. "Carly," he said softly.

When I kissed him back, it was with everything I felt. Jack stopped laughing; I could feel him trembling up and down.

Empty gray gymnasiums are good places to kiss as well as to pray in. I don't know how long we stayed wrapped in each other's arms. At last I said, "I, uh, guess we should get back to the office."

Jack nodded and let go of me.

But as soon as the basketball was put away, he pulled me close again and kept his arm around me all the way to the student center.

"Are my cheeks as red as they feel?" I asked.

Jack grinned. "Like apples," he said.

"Everybody's going to be a little surprised about you and me, don't you think?"

"Well, maybe not Anna," he replied, "but the others will be. I don't think Hau has a clue, and I know Harry doesn't. We're both pretty good fakers," he added, as we walked down the hall. A note was posted on the office door. Jack kissed me once more before we read it.

> Dear Carly & Jack,
>   Couldn't stay any longer. Everyone's meeting at Pizza Palace 6:30 to celebrate. See you there.
>
>   Harry
> P.S. Hau told Heather you went on the school bus with the kids, and it might be hours before you both returned.
> P.P.S. Don't let me down, guys. I love a happy ending.

Do you ever wonder about falling in love? About members of the opposite sex? Do you need a little friendly advice but have no one to turn to? Well, that's where we come in . . . Jenny and Jake. Send us those questions you're dying to ask, and we'll give you the straight scoop on life and love in the nineties.

DEAR JAKE

Q: *I'm pretty close with a guy named Ryder. You might even say I have a major crush on him. But today I found out that Ryder's van almost went off a cliff last night. Everyone's saying that he was drunk and that all his friends were drunk too. I think Ryder has a big problem with alcohol. And he's failing all his classes too. I'm afraid that if I bring up the subject, he'll tell me to mind my own business. I'm worried about his safety and I don't want to lose his friendship. I'd like for us to become more than friends eventually. Should I get involved or just keep my big mouth shut?*

MF, Myrtle Beach, SC

A: No one can solve another person's problems. It sounds as if Ryder has a lot of things he needs to work out on his own. You're right to be worried about his safety. Drinking and driving can be deadly. But it's up to Ryder to make his own decisions about the way he lives his life.

If you really care about him, definitely express your concern. He might be hurt or defensive when you bring up the topic, so approach him as gently as you can. Tell him that you're worried his drinking may be out of control. If he can't handle the discussion, back off. And if you don't feel comfortable keeping silent, talk with a counselor or your favorite teacher about your fears. Remember, your number one responsibility is to yourself and you should never allow concern for someone else's needs to override your own. You deserve a boyfriend who will respect himself and others. Ryder needs to learn to take care of himself before he can even come close to making you happy.

Q: *Joey and I dated two years ago. We were happy for a while . . . until I broke up with him. I just didn't want to be tied to one person. I've dated lots of guys since then, but none of them have measured up to Joey. For almost a year now I've felt that the breakup was a mistake. I want him back!*

Sometimes Joey's friendly, and we still joke around together, but other times he acts as if he doesn't even know me. I think he's afraid of getting hurt again. I know now that I messed up majorly when I broke up with Joey. Do you think I have a chance of getting him back?
LY, Keller, TX

A: Joey has every reason to be wary of further romantic involvement with you. He's been burned by you once, so why should he take the risk of being burned again? If you really want him back, you'll need to do some serious baring of your soul. A little begging won't hurt either. And even then, Joey may have already decided that it's time to move on.

So before you plan your full-scale telephone and love-note campaign, make sure that you don't want Joey for all the wrong reasons. When you look back on a relationship, it's easy to forget the bad and remember only the good. Obviously, everything wasn't perfect or you wouldn't have broken up in the first place. Are you sure the reasons for your last breakup won't still be important to you now? If so, be honest with Joey. That way, both of you can move into this new phase of your relationship with your eyes wide open.

DEAR JENNY

Q: *Over winter vacation my family went to Paris. I met a boy there and we fell in love. He's Australian and I'm Brazilian, and the only way we can communicate is through the mail and the Internet. My family doesn't approve of our relationship and they won't stop bugging me about it. They think that romances with foreigners are doomed to failure. But I think that Matt and I have a chance and I'm willing to take the risk. How do I get my family to back off?*
AH, Rio de Janeiro, Brazil

A: Your family is upset because they know how hard a long-distance relationship can be. And when your boyfriend is from a different culture, that can make it even harder to communicate and understand each other. But they have to realize that you are your own person.

Sit down with your family and listen to their concerns. Tell them that you take their worries seriously and that you are grateful for their love and support. If they know that you've heard what they have to say, maybe they'll feel as if they've managed to prepare you for what this relationship might offer.

After you've heard them out, think over what they've

said. If you still want to commit to the relationship with Matt, tell them gently that this is your life, and that you feel you are responsible enough to make your own decisions. Remember though, boyfriends come and go, but your family is forever.

Q: *Last September I met this gorgeous guy at school and it was love at first sight. We flirted a lot at first and then he asked me out. Even though everyone at school knew he was a player, I accepted the date. I felt that we had something special. We dated for about a month, and then I found out that he was cheating on me. It totally broke my heart.*

Now he's become part of my clique, so we hang out together a lot as friends. But I'm afraid I'm falling in love with him all over again. My best friend says she can tell he still likes me. I don't want to lose my heart a second time, but I can't deny my feelings much longer. What should I do?

PD, Indianapolis, IN

A: This is a really tough situation. It makes it that much harder to get over someone if you're constantly hanging out together. No wonder your feelings for him are still intense. You need to step back from this scene and get some perspective. Maybe instead of going out with the whole gang, you can hang with just a few good friends at a time, giving your feelings a chance to settle down.

After a breakup, everyone feels confused and vulnerable. Suddenly all the energy you've invested in your boyfriend or girlfriend has to be turned somewhere else. Your ex probably *does* care about you, especially since you're friends. But that doesn't mean that the two of you should be together. A guy who cheats after just one month isn't boyfriend material. You deserve a respectful, committed relationship, and it seems that he just wants to fool around. This combination is a recipe for heartbreak. I know it's hard, but letting go now is the only way you can clear the path for the true love of your life, a guy who will do everything he can to make you happy.

Do you have questions about love? Write to:

Jenny Burgess or Jake Korman
c/o Daniel Weiss Associates
33 West 17th Street
New York, NY 10011